Unequaled

No Rival, 3

Charity Parkerson

--Warning: This book is intended for readers over the age of 18.

Editor: Vicky Reese
Photographer: Dariyad & Zamuruev
Originally published by Ellora's Cave Publishing
under the same title.
ISBN-10:1-946099-03-1
ISBN-13:978-1-946099-03-7

Introduction

No Rival, book 3

Kerry has hated Rhys from the moment she set eyes on him. They've never had an encounter that didn't end with them both enraged. Paired up at his brother's wedding, their clashing personalities come to a head and a daring wager is made. Rhys agrees to submit to Kerry for a single evening if she will do the same. Considering the sexual flavors Rhys has enjoyed in his past, it's one bet Rhys is sure he can't lose. But Kerry has a few secrets of her own and her plans for him land Rhys in a place he never expected— the arms of sexy Italian solicitor, Asher D'Ettore.

Asher becomes an obsession Rhys can't

shake. His alpha ways and confident mannerisms render all of Rhys' usual charm useless. With his hard-earned reputation in the media spotlight, Rhys is forced to make a choice between his public persona and true love.

Dedication

For Helle Gade. You're the best Beta Reader in the world. Thank you for not killing me when Rhys wouldn't settle down.

Chapter One

She almost made it to her car before he called her name. "Where are you headed?"

Taking note of the dark smudges beneath Dane's eyes, Kerry did her best to convince herself he needed rest. Most likely, he'd not slept since his brother, Knox's accident, maybe even since way before then. "I thought about grabbing something to eat and possibly picking up a movie." She shrugged. "Nothing special."

There was something about him. She couldn't look away. His eyes hooded and his features tightened. A tingle flared to life between her legs. Holy hell. He'd gotten her wet in a single glance.

"You should come home with me instead. I promise you won't get bored."

His arms hung loosely at his sides. Not a single hint of hesitation tainted his offer for a night she would never forget. The memory of silken restraints tugging at her wrists as his hot mouth closed around her nipple flashed across her mind. The prickle of need pulsing at her clit intensified. A tiny smirk hovered on his lips. He knew.

"Do you regret me?"

She couldn't lie. "Not for one damn minute."

The smirk transformed into a full-fledged mocking grin at her admission. "You won't this time either," he promised. She didn't doubt his words for a second. Dane Collier was the sexual equivalent of a no-spending-limit shoe shopping expedition mixed with a tub full of guilt-free chocolate. She would rock his fucking world.

* * * * *

The copper tang of blood coated Rhys'

tongue. His muscles burned. Fire raced down one leg. It couldn't be anything good causing such a pain, but he didn't have time to worry about it. Terry Richards was going down. No doubt about it, the dude had gotten some good shots in, but Rhys hadn't come this far to lose now. Tunnel vision took over. Bouncing on his toes, he moved in, cracking Terry across the cheekbone. It was only a graze. It didn't faze him, but it did count as another point in Rhys' favor.

Terry was only five-foot-ten, but he was built like a bull. Red-haired with the famous temper to match, Terry had held the title for a long time, but Rhys had earned his chance to face-off against him. If he couldn't knock the bastard out, Rhys knew he could damn well beat him in scoring. Lowering his shoulder, Terry tackled him. Even though Rhys saw it coming, the impact caught him in the sternum. Air lodged in Rhys' throat forcing its way out in a whoosh as his back smacked the mat. Terry's emotions were getting the best of him. It was the break Rhys had been waiting for. With his head unprotected, Terry had to choose between keeping Rhys pinned down or allowing blows to rain down on him. Rhys got several punches in before Terry's grip slackened. From this angle, Rhys couldn't throw much weight behind the jabs, but it was all about the points. Patience. He was slowly leaning things in his favor.

Exhaustion weighed on his muscles as heavily as Terry. A solid hit to the side of Terry's head gave Rhys the freedom to scramble away. Sucking air, he desperately sought enough oxygen to support his system. Sweat stung his eyes. He could barely feel a thing past the adrenaline. Endorphins poured through his system. He'd lost his hearing several minutes ago under the rush. Terry's stance wavered. Without a thought, Rhys' instincts kicked in and he struck. Flesh dug into his knee as it sank into Terry's gut. The bones in his right arm vibrated at the impact of his strike to the man's jaw. Points no longer mattered once Terry went down.

The noise of the crowd roared back to life inside his head. The switch from resounding silence to ear-piercing noise reminded Rhys of all the times he'd left the stereo blaring in his truck only to get blown away the next time he fired it up. His reaction was the same, as well. His heart slammed against his chest with enough force to rock him on his feet. Even as his arm rose in victory, the dreamlike trance coating his brain didn't dissipate.

The emptiness inside him also lingered. It seemed even winning the world wasn't enough.

* * * * *

"I know you're busy, or hell, maybe you're just avoiding me, but I need to talk to you." A long pause followed Knox's words, but Rhys knew he was still there. He couldn't delete the message until he knew it all. When Knox finally spoke again, Rhys was left feeling a bit deflated. "Just call me, or something."

What had he expected? An apology? Rhys snorted at the idea. That day would never come. Skipping ahead, he listened to another message from Knox. It was almost identical to the last. By the time he made it to the third voicemail, he expected it to be more or less the same. Mandy's voice rang through the line. Everything inside him froze at the sweet sound. His chest tightened. Even the noise of the overcrowded bar couldn't take away from the beauty of it. "I'd like to think you're not ignoring us, but I know better." She laughed. There wasn't a hint of humor in it. It didn't matter. He still wanted more. "Please don't shut out Knox because of me. I love you both so much. It breaks my heart to think of you hurting each other. Here's the deal. Our wedding is in two weeks. Knox wants to ask you to be at his side, but you won't answer his calls. I know he would be upset if he knew I'd called you about it, but if you're not there, it'll kill us both. Please do this for me?"

Rhys slumped against the bar and replayed the message. He was man enough to admit Knox hadn't stolen anything from him. He'd lost Mandy all on his own. There wasn't an off switch for his feelings. A tall redhead lingered nearby.

The glances she cast in his direction left no doubt about her intentions. Showing her his back, Rhys listened to Mandy's words one more time, attempting to picture her face. She seemed so far away.

He didn't have anything scheduled for a while. Tapping the phone against his thigh, he tossed back the last of his Jack and Coke. He needed to go home.

* * * * *

He was a glutton for punishment. It was the only reasonable explanation as to why Rhys chose to come to Grid Iron. He could have called or dropped by Knox's house, but some things needed to be done in person. Reappearing after eight months of hiding, while avoiding his brother's attempts to reach him, was one of those things. He also could not pass up the chance to torment Kerry. That was if she even still worked there. Kerry Crawford was the only woman in Rhys' memory who had ever hated him on sight. Under normal circumstances, Rhys would have found a way to charm her out of the unwarranted feelings of animosity she held over him. She wanted none of it. Their paths never crossed without an argument breaking out. He wasn't sure what it was about the tiny brown-haired woman that pushed all his buttons. Whatever it was, he couldn't give her an inch. Apparently, the feeling was mutual. Unfortunately, her position at Grid Iron Fitness Club—where Knox worked out each day—made it impossible for Rhys to breach the joint without her raining her evil down on his head. Today, he relished the thought of a good fight.

At the first sight of her sitting behind the check-in counter, a burst of happiness went through him. He chalked the feeling up to a sinful sense of glee. These days, there wasn't much of anything he took pleasure in. Unfortunately, she barely glanced his way. Not even a hint of surprise over his appearance crossed her face. The closer he came to her the more he realized something was wrong.

Staring straight ahead with a flushed face and a fine sheen of sweat covering her skin, Kerry looked ready to pass out.

"Are you running a fever?"

Her eyes were glassy and unfocused. "What?"

The tiny crease between her brows spoke volumes about her confusion. He wondered if she was delirious. "You're red-faced and I can hear you struggling to breathe. How long have you been this sick?"

"I'll be fine," she croaked out.

The lack of concern over her well-being pissed him off. Anything was better than concentrating on the real reason for his visit.

"Seriously, Kerry? You need to go home—or better yet, to the doctor. Yet you're sitting here spreading your germs to everyone who comes in this place." Getting up on his soapbox, Rhys' ire rose. "You know, you're one of those people who never considers anyone other than yourself." She gripped the edge of the desk, knuckles whitening as she visibly swallowed. "Shit. Are you going to throw up? Have you even thought about the people who work out here? What if they're caring for an elderly parent or a child with a weak immune system? For Christ's sake, Kerry."

She shoved a laminated card across

the counter with the words "temporary pass" stamped across it. "Just go." Her barked words sounded as if they hurt her throat. Holding the card between his thumb and forefinger as if it were poisonous, he snapped his teeth together to bite off further lecture. She pointed at the door. Doing as she bade, he pushed through the glass doorway separating the club from the foyer before she could change her mind. He fought the urge to pat himself on the back. When he made it out of there with his skin intact, then he'd celebrate. Kerry had never let him off so easily. Her scathing insults were legendary.

*

Kerry's nether lips parted under the pressure of Dane's tongue. He teased the sensitized bud hidden there. Relentlessly, her channel pulsed beneath the onslaught

18

of his ministrations. Rhys had horrible fucking timing. As always. An orgasm rocked Kerry as the glass door swept closed behind him.

"Oh my God."

A deep rumble of laughter drifted out from underneath the desk. "Is he gone?"

"Holy hell." Her muscles shook. Dane closed his lips around her clit, sucking hard.

A second wave of ecstasy ripped through her, proving he was still the master of oral sex. He hummed against her pussy.

"Delicious." With one last stroke to draw out as much pleasure as possible, he pressed his face against her thigh for a moment. Kerry could almost feel him attempting to call his body under control. "I love this skirt," he said after a moment.

"It's very accommodating."

"I'll never be able to wear it again without thinking of you, that's for sure." Pushing the chair away from the desk, she made room for him to climb out from his hiding spot. On his knees, he clasped her thighs between his hands and yanked her forward.

"You're an evil woman."

Riding the high of pleasure, she chose to embrace his words. If he thought she was evil, she could show him wicked.

"How hard are you right now?"

He groaned. Burying his face against the side of her neck, he pretended to cry. "So fucking hard."

It was mean. She giggled. "My poor baby."

"You'll pay for this. You realize that, right?" Dane pushed to his feet even as he made the threat. The line of his erection showed clearly through his jeans. A shiver of anticipation ran through her.

"Promise?"

His blue eyes darkened at her question. "Will you play nice with my baby brother while he's in town?"

Taking note of the worry in his tone, Kerry did her best to stamp down any irritation over the question. How could he doubt her?

"I'll be good." Huh. She didn't sound like a petulant child after all. Go her.

"You'll make him feel welcome?" Dane added. She rolled her eyes. It happened before she could stop it. So much for being an adult. Oh well. She'd tried.

"I will make him feel welcome," she repeated dutifully.

Dane eyed her as if trying to decide if she was telling the truth. The corners of his mouth turned up, twisting into a mocking grin. "You're so going to pay."

Her gaze moved from his mussed blond hair to the flush of arousal on his cheeks before coming to rest on his lips. She couldn't wait.

* * * * *

Rhys almost didn't recognize his brother. Knox's once shaggy hair had been cut military short. He looked younger. Laugh lines formed at the corners of Knox's eyes as he spoke to the bleach-blond guy spotting the weights above him.

"You called."

Carefully, Knox lifted the weight bar, set it back in its holder and sat up. The smile remained in place. He didn't show even a hint of surprise over Rhys' sudden reappearance. It was as if they'd seen each other yesterday instead of months ago. "A few times as I recall."

Rhys shifted uncomfortably even though there hadn't been any hint of accusation in his brother's tone. "I've been busy." It was true. He had been training for and participating in back to back matches for the past eight months. Of course, he could have taken five minutes to call. He'd chosen not to.

"I've heard. Congratulations on the title win. Middleweight champion is a huge deal."

The surprise must have shown on Rhys' face because Knox's grin grew. "What? Did you think I wouldn't keep up with you? I always have."

Damned if Knox's statement didn't move Rhys from the absentee brother category into the asshole bracket in a heartbeat.

"How's Mandy?"

"Doing good. Taking over the world

with a smile. You know how she does. Nothing has changed there." In a shift of topics, Knox asked, "Where are you staying while you're town? We'd love for you to come and stay with us."

Rhys honestly had not meant the question about Mandy as a dick move. Unfortunately, it felt like one leaving his lips. In the light of Knox's offer, the feeling doubled. It shouldn't be this way between them. The uncomfortable feeling grew. Stay with them? Was he kidding?

"So, you called."

Knox cast a glance over his shoulder at the spotter who was still hanging out behind him. At the look, the man walked away, leaving them alone. "Yeah. I don't know if you've heard or not, but our wedding is this coming weekend. Mandy wants you there." He paused for a second before adding, "Also, I'd really like to have you standing there by my side. I know it's probably the last thing in the world you want to do, but you're my brother."

Glancing away from Knox's hopeful stare, Rhys watched the other patrons moving from machine to machine. They were going about their exercise routines with no idea they stood mere feet from a man who was dying inside. His older brother was days away from marrying the woman Rhys always believed would one day be his wife. This was why Rhys had left this fucking town. Eight months earlier, Knox had almost been killed in a car accident. When he'd woken up from his coma, Rhys had walked out of the hospital, packed up all his worldly goods and gotten the hell out while the getting was good. He hadn't looked back. Too bad those months had done nothing to bridge the gap between them.

"Getting married, huh?" Rhys said, in an attempt to buy his brain some time to work.

"That's not what I said. I said our wedding is this coming weekend. Mandy and I got married the day after I was released from the hospital. This is only a formality."

"Wow. I'm speechless." Rhys still couldn't look at Knox. He truly was without words. Even knowing in advance why Knox wanted to speak with him had not prepared him for this conversation. He'd shown up. Maybe it would count for something.

Knox made a sound somewhere between a growl and a sigh. "Look, Rhys. I'm sorry for how things turned out between us, but I can't and won't apologize for anything with Mandy. Someday, someone will look at you the way she looks

26

at me. You'll be instantly addicted to how it makes you feel. When that day comes, I hope you'll forgive me for my complete inability to let her go."

His words closely mimicked the ones Kerry had said to him while Knox had been hospitalized. Rhys hated her a little for it. The thought of Kerry reminded him of something else important. He spotted Ryan across the room.

"You were forgiven a long time ago," he said absently before adding. "I'll be back in a second. I need to speak to Ryan real quick."

Knox nodded and waved his spotter back over as Rhys wandered away. He caught up with Ryan before he could lose him. "Hey, man. Can I talk to you for a minute?"

A friendly smile lit Ryan's face as he reached out to shake Rhys' hand. "Of course. How have you been? I haven't seen you around in a while."

Accepting Ryan's handshake, Rhys answered his question. "I'm doing good. Hey, I know it's none of my business, but have you seen Kerry today? She looks like hell. I think she may be running a temperature."

A hint of worry touched Ryan's features. He quickly strode to the door between the club and foyer, peering through the glass. "She looks okay to me."

Rhys moved to flank him and peeked out, as well. Kerry chatted cheerfully with a deliveryman who looked a bit too happy to have her attention focused on him. Dane leaned against the wall behind her flipping through a magazine. "Well, that's odd. Maybe it was only me, then."

Ryan nodded. "You do seem to bring

out a different side of her." Even though Ryan chuckled as he spoke, Rhys could hear the questioning note in his voice.

Instead of dredging up his grudge with the man's sister, Rhys said, "Dane is here. I didn't even see him when I came in, but then again, he's always been good at blending into the background."

"I imagine it's a survival mechanism for him."

"Hmm," Rhys said noncommittally since he didn't understand how going unnoticed helped Dane. "Well, I guess since Kerry appears fine now, I'll let you get on with your day."

Ryan started away then hesitated before stopping Rhys. "I never got the chance to thank you for what you did for Max. I realize it wasn't your intention to help us by outing him with Drew, but honestly, it lifted a huge weight off his shoulders, so thank you."

Without waiting for a response, he strode away. Rhys watched him go, feeling a little better about himself. When Max's father had passed away, Rhys had gone to the funeral services with Max's brother Drew. Afterward, he'd inadvertently witnessed a private moment between Ryan and Max. When their secret affair stood in the way of him leaving the gathering, he'd simply stated the pair were in love. He never meant to hurt anyone. He'd known Drew would embrace their relationship. Ryan was right in thinking it also had not been his intention to help them, but in a way, he'd hoped it would. Not everyone was as lucky as Ryan and Max, which reminded Rhys of why he was there. Apparently, he would stand behind his brother while he said his vows to the woman Rhys loved. Yep. Not everyone got lucky. With a sigh, he went to share the good news with Knox.

* * * * *

With his bag in hand and his heart on his sleeve, Rhys rapped his knuckles on the wood door. He'd waffled for close to three hours before ending up here. Of course, now he almost wished he had made a different choice. The light-colored stone walls and massive windows, which allowed for a clear view all the way through the house to the pool out back, didn't give away a hint as to whether or not the owner was at home. Part of him hoped she wasn't. However, Mandy's smile changed his mind as soon as she opened the door. He couldn't remember the last time she'd been happy to see him.

"Rhys!" The excited squeal of his name was the only warning she gave before throwing herself at him. As her

31

body slammed against him and her arms encircled his neck, he shifted his hips away expecting his stupid dick to go hard at the first brush of her skin. She'd always had that effect on him. Her sweet smell engulfed him. Nothing. Huh.

He squeezed her tighter. "Missed you." His confession came out sounding hoarse, but even as she stepped away, her grin remained in place.

"I've missed you too. Have you decided to stay with us, after all?" she asked, motioning toward his bag. Up until the words left her mouth, he had not been sure Knox's offer had been a genuine one, but he'd obviously talked it over with Mandy at some point. He wasn't even sure why he was there. What did he hope to gain besides torturing himself?

"Um. Yeah. I don't know how long I'll be in town. I thought it might be a good idea to spend as much time with you as I can before I head out again."

Her face fell at the mention of him leaving. She dropped her gaze in an obvious attempt to hide her reaction as she moved aside. "I didn't mean to leave you standing in the doorway. Come in. All the upstairs bedrooms are still empty so you can have your pick. Knox is asleep, but I know he'll be thrilled when he learns you've decided to stay here."

Rhys' steps faltered. "Knox is asleep? As in taking a nap, asleep?"

A giggle escaped Mandy. "Go put your stuff away and get back here. I want to hear all about what you've been doing."

Upon her order, he rushed up the staircase. Choosing the first open doorway at the top, he tossed his bag on the queen-sized bed. Knox's house had always been nice. Now, everywhere Rhys looked, he could see how Mandy had turned the place into a home. Rhys understood completely what Knox got in Mandy as he eyed the deep maroon bedspread and gleaming wooden furniture. This place felt like a safe haven where children could be raised in peace while surrounded by love. Damned if Rhys' nose didn't sting at the thought. Knox and Mandy deserved this life. They were both good. Leaving his envy behind, Rhys made his way back down the stairs.

Taking his time, he paused to look at a few of the photos hanging on the walls along the way. Mandy's job as a professional photographer for a sports magazine gave her an outlet for her passion. Her love for it showed in the images. One in particular, right inside the den, drew his eye. He moved to inspect it closer. With the camera held at arm's length, Mandy had snapped a picture of Knox and her together. Knox's hand splayed across her cheek as if he'd forced her face to turn his way. They stared into each other's eyes. The contrasts between his scarred knuckles and her delicate features were vast. A black titanium wedding band encircled Knox's ring finger. Rhys hadn't noticed it at Grid Iron, but at the time, fingerless weightlifting gloves covered Knox's hands. There was something about the image. He couldn't look away.

"It's hardly studio quality, but it's one of my favorites."

At the sound of Mandy's voice, he glanced behind him to find her sitting on the couch. He'd not seen her there when he'd entered the room. Neither had he looked.

"It's an amazing shot," he admitted

as he proceeded to sit next to her. Blonde-haired, blue-eyed, willowy and nearly six feet in height, Mandy was beyond gorgeous. However, the most beautiful thing about her was her heart. To hear Mandy tell it, when she looked in the mirror, she saw a woman with no curves who towered over every man she met. Rhys hoped Knox had managed to convince her otherwise.

"I take it you're still enjoying your job at the magazine," Rhys added, for lack of anything else to talk about.

"I am, and look at you, Middleweight Champion. How does it feel? Have you finally proven to yourself you're worthy of the position?"

There it was, the reason he'd been unable to let her go when he should have. She understood. "The million-dollar question," he mused, causing her to release frustrated growl.

"Come on, Rhys. Your dad has been gone for over a year now. Surely, you can admit you didn't need his name to succeed. It was all you."

He couldn't help but laugh at her outrage. "Yes. In the end, it was only me."

At his admission, her face lit. Everything in his mind cleared away. She was his friend. Damn, he really didn't want to lose that. Luckily, Knox's arrival saved him from making an ass of himself by begging her not to steal her friendship away from him.

"I thought I heard voices." He leaned over the back of the couch and kissed Mandy before giving Rhys his full attention. "Are you here for a visit or did you change your mind about staying with us for a while?"

"You know I'm too cheap to spring

for a hotel." Before Knox could make a big deal of it, Rhys changed the subject. "What's up with you sleeping during the day? Are you finally ready to admit you're getting old?"

Knox chuckled as he pulled Mandy to her feet. Claiming her seat, he settled her back down in his lap. "Yeah man. You know what they say, naps are for children and the elderly. I'm sure no child," he tacked on with a wink.

Damned if seeing them together didn't make everything okay. They were happy. "So, I missed the actual wedding, huh?"

"You and everyone else," Knox said, answering his question. "It was just us and a really bad Elvis impersonator."

Rhys snorted before it occurred to him Knox might be serious. "Are you joking?"

"Nope." After a moment, Knox added cheerfully. "I figured we may as well make the occasion as memorable as possible."

Rhys could only shake his head. "What's happened to you?" He wanted to bite off his own tongue. The question had fallen from his lips before he could call it back. He knew the answer, of course, but the changes in his brother were nothing short of miraculous.

"I'm getting married."

Rhys felt moved to point out the obvious at Knox's answer. "You're already married."

Knox shrugged. "It's impossible to marry Mandy too many times."

"Awww," Mandy drawled happily.

"This is a bit sickening." With a resigned sigh, Rhys added, "I'm assuming I've missed all the rehearsal stuff. Am I throwing this whole wedding party off with my arrival?"

"Of course not!" Mandy's immediate outraged denial was overshadowed by Knox's dark scowl.

"You're my brother. You can throw off as much shit as you'd like, but if you're worried about missing rehearsal, don't. I'm sure you know how to hold a girl's arm and walk down a damn aisle."

Knox's defense on his behalf had Rhys determined to put his best face on. "Awesome. Bridesmaids," he said cheerfully, rubbing his hands together. "Who do I get?"

Mandy clapped happily. "I'm pairing you with Kerry."

For a moment, Rhys thought he might have blacked out. Luckily, it passed quickly. "Great." Even as the word left his lips, he marveled over how calm he sounded. Turned out he was getting better at lying all the time.

The days leading up to the wedding passed in an amazing blur of activity. It seemed his arrival, while not throwing things completely out of balance, had forced a rush on Mandy's backup plan. Since she'd hoped he would eventually accept, a cousin on her mother's side planned to add her presence to the wedding party for the march down the aisle. Dane landed the spot of best man. Rhys didn't begrudge him the honor. He had been the one who stuck around. When the music signaled the start of the ceremony, Rhys did everything he could think of to keep from looking directly at Mandy as she walked toward the brother who'd won her. The cream color of her gown fell across her tan skin to perfection. His fingers clenched. Not his, he reminded himself, forcing his

41

hands to relax. He focused on some spot above her head instead.

Halfway through Mandy repeating her vows, the truth struck Rhys with a sudden blow to the gut. It didn't matter that they were already married. Witnessing it happen made everything real. His spine stiffened. Mandy would never belong to him. His heart hardened. She was his sister by marriage now. His heart shattered. Rhys almost thought he heard the pieces breaking apart.

Somehow, he made it to the very end. Out of the corner of his eye, he could see Kerry casting nervous glances in his direction as if expecting he would make a scene. It pissed him off. There was enough anger building inside him to level the building around them. It needed an outlet. When it came time to kiss the bride, the rowdy bunch of degenerate fighters sitting at their backs exploded into raunchy cheers. Knox raised a clenched fist above his head even as he deepened their kiss.

Rhys' eyes fell closed, blocking out the vision of happiness they presented. He swallowed hard. A warm weight settled on his arm. Glancing down, he took note of the painted and manicured nails resting on his dark coat sleeve. They blurred for a moment. He took a deep breath, forcing his eyes to focus.

"You did a good thing. It's almost over," Kerry promised him, pitching her voice low. He dipped his chin, letting her know he'd heard. What felt like an eternity later, Rhys escorted Kerry back down the aisle. Several pink flower petals scattered across the white runner. Rhys intentionally focused on them while forcing his lips to shape a smile. At least, he hoped he was smiling and not grimacing. The reception hall came into view. His gaze landed on a pyramid of champagne glasses with golden liquid flowing down the sides. Thank God. There would be alcohol.

At the last moment, Kerry stepped into an open doorway to the right tugging him inside, as well. Since his brain had gone numb several minutes earlier, he could only glance around uncaring of his surroundings as Kerry pulled the door closed behind them.

Handbags, shoes and bags full of clothing scattered across a beige settee. Mirrors covered two of the walls. Makeup lined a counter nearby. Rhys absently noted it must have been where the bridal party had gotten ready before the wedding. Kerry leaned her back against the closed door. She didn't say a word. Instead, she watched him steadily as if expecting him to snap at any time. Her brown hair, which usually brushed her chin, was now pinned tightly behind her head. It made her green eyes seem larger than normal. Thankfully, there didn't seem to be any pity inside them, only understanding. He couldn't get a good read on her. Kerry had always been a puzzle to him. She shifted nervously when he didn't look away, making him wonder what she saw in his face.

He dropped his gaze to the dark pink dress she wore. He imagined the color had a name, but he didn't know it. All he knew was it was sleeveless. Kerry's generous curves looked amazing. Each breath she took gave men hope she would spill over the top.

"Ah, there is the Rhys I know. You had me worried for a minute."

"I have no idea why you would think of me at all much less worry."

"You're a bad liar."

"I don't do it often," he said honestly.

She tilted her head to one side, searching his face with her eyes. "You really don't, do you?"

He shrugged. Some feeling returned to his brain. "I don't care for liars so I try not to be one."

"I'm sorry."

Her apology caught him off guard. "For what?"

"For not believing you were in love with her."

She didn't need to expound on her answer. It's not as if she could be talking about anyone else. There had only been one "her" for him. Before Rhys had left town, Kerry had been adamant in her belief Rhys could not possibly be in love with Mandy. Backtracking went against

Kerry's nature. It made him uncomfortable.

"I'm not."

"I thought you hated liars."

"I've let her go."

Kerry sneered. "Damn. It's getting worse."

"I have to let her go," Rhys said, sounding desperate even to his ears.

"Yes. You do."

He wanted to hate her for agreeing. He wanted to hurt her for knowing too much, for being honest. Powerless to stop it from happening, he could feel his lips twisting into a smirk. Her eyes flashed in challenge, daring him.

Doing his best to piss her off, he added as much scorn to his tone as possible. "It's finally occurred to me why it is you don't like me." He paused, allowing his words to seep in. "You can't stand the fact you're attracted to me." The look on her face was priceless. It was a mixture of horror and outrage. Unfortunately, once the initial satisfaction passed, it stung his pride. It also didn't bring anywhere near the satisfaction he thought it would.

"You must be joking. I would eat you alive then send you home with a limp and a juice box. You're nowhere near freaky enough to keep pace with me."

Her opinion of him caused Rhys to snort. It also piqued his curiosity. "Me? You seriously think I couldn't keep up with you? There's not much I haven't done at some point, so I seriously doubt it. Not to mention, you're so controlling. I find it hard to believe you have any kink in you at all. One night of submitting to me would ruin you for anyone else."

"Is that a challenge?"

His body hummed. He couldn't

remember the last time he felt this alive. He also recognized how she'd twisted his hurt into something else. An unexpected surge of respect ran through him. She was more like her brother than he'd realized. The flush on her skin drew his gaze. He allowed it to sweep over her. Lingering on the strategic places, his mouth watered. His cock lengthened when her hard nipples showed through the satin material of her dress. She was turned on. An image of her bent over the velvet settee flashed across his mind. A growl rose in his throat. He swallowed it down.

"What if it is?"

Her eyes became calculating at his question. "What about an exchange? I will agree to submit to you for one night, if you agree to the same terms."

The muscles in his stomach clenched. His cock twitched. He would have her. In his satisfaction over the idea, he almost agreed immediately. Thankfully, at the last second, he stopped. "How will we know who the winner is and what is the prize?"

A sinful smile touched her lips. "Whoever cries uncle first is the loser. As for a prize, I'm content with besting you. Oh, not to mention being able to lord it over you for the rest of your life."

Striding over to the spot between the mirror and doorway, he leaned his shoulder against the wall. Rhys crossed his arms over his chest pretending nonchalance. A list of depraved things ran through his mind. This would be fun.

"Who goes first?" Keeping up the questions instead of fucking her right then was a challenge.

"You're right, of course," she admitted with a sigh. "We need to find a fair way to decide."

"Coin toss?"

He'd meant it as a joke, but she nodded. "Seems fair," she said, moving to snag her purse from the table next to the couch. He had change in his pocket. However, retrieving it meant missing out on watching her ass as she crossed the room. She would beg for mercy. Holding up a quarter for his inspection, Kerry paused to clarify the rules. "No strings. We do this safe. No tears when I break your heart." On the heels of her jab, she tossed the coin in the air, adding, "Call it."

"Heads," Rhys said before it could hit the floor. He stared, transfixed as the metal piece spun on its side before toppling over, tails up. Even having lost the coin toss, a silky chuckle fell from his lips. "No tears when you can't get me out of your head."

"Juice box and a limp," she repeated each syllable slowly. "Do you know where Skyway Mall is on Farley?" At his nod, an evil grin touched her mouth. "Be there at nine tonight. Don't be late. I don't like to be kept waiting."

Rhys watched her slip out through the door unable to work up an ounce of regret over losing the coin toss.

* * * * *

Dane would kill her. Dead. She was dead. The only thing Kerry could do was pray she could reach Asher before it came time to confess her sins. Clutching her purse to her chest, she headed for the parking lot, hoping against hope no one noticed her absence. Dane would, but she needed privacy to make this call. Behind the wheel of her car, she took a deep breath and scrolled through her contact list. With the phone pressed to her ear, her heart rate didn't slow until the deep accent poured through the line. A bit of feeling returned to her numb limbs. She would fix this. Rhys' devastated expression as he watched Mandy marry his brother flashed across her mind. She would make everything right.

Chapter Two

She chose a red satin dress for her date with Rhys. Sometime between the reception and their scheduled meeting, calm settled over her. Anticipation set in. This was her territory. Familiar ground. Skyway Mall was home to some of the most upscale stores in the area. They each locked their doors promptly at six on Sunday night. No one who glanced at the darkened building this late in the evening would ever suspect the things going on just below the surface.

Headlights reflected in the glass storefront as Rhys pulled in alongside her. The F150 fell silent. Its driver spilled out. Her pulse quickened. The wide shoulders and narrow hips moving in her direction drew an involuntary growl from the back of her throat. It was ridiculous for any one person to be as sexy as Rhys Collier. The closer he came, the more her muscles tensed. Her territory, she reminded herself. The door opened and his hand appeared in front of her. Even as his warm fingers closed around hers, Kerry wondered if she could go through with this.

It was too late. Once her feet hit the pavement and his clean scent filled her lungs, her nipples hardened. She glanced at his sexy brown eyes and full bottom lip. Her gaze skittered away.

"It's not too late to back down." The deep rumble of his voice rolled down her back and made her wonder if her thoughts were written all over her face. She did want to run. Instead, she forced her eyes to move away from the wide expanse of his hard chest back to his face. Half-lidded eyes, which held more than a hint of lust, met hers. Her breasts felt heavy.

"You're right. It's not too late for you to throw in the towel."

His nostrils flared. "Not a chance."

"Then let the games begin," she said, slamming her car door behind her. Wrapping her fingers around his upper arm, Kerry tried desperately to concentrate on putting one foot in front of the other instead of the way his arm felt as hard as marble. Holy shit. It was truly unfair. It really was. Drawing him closer, she headed straight for the darkened building.

"Looks closed to me."

"Hmm," Kerry said noncommittally. She could feel the curiosity rolling off him in waves but didn't bother to ease it. His muscles tensed beneath her fingertips. Moisture flooded her channel at the thought of his powerful body underneath her.

"Good evening." At the sound of Kurt's soft voice floating out of the darkness, she realized he was the cause of Rhys' reaction.

"Hey, Kurt. How's it going?" Kerry hoped her familiarity with the man would ease Rhys' concerns. The Collier brothers did tend to strike first and ask questions later.

A flash of white teeth appeared before Kurt returned to his usual stoic expression. His huge frame, dark scowl, menacing head-to-toe tattoos and unusual piercings were enough to keep most people at bay. However, Kerry wasn't most people. Dragging Rhys forward and closing the distance between them, she attempted a quick one-arm hug. The giant had other plans. Snagging her from Rhys' protection, her toes left the ground. The air whooshed from her lungs on a squeak as he squeezed her against his chest.

"Fresh," she accused without any real heat when he set her away. His green eyes twinkled with humor.

"If your friend wasn't already raring to kick my ass, I'd show you fresh. I promise you'd never forget it, darling."

She had no doubt. Kerry's mind went a bit fuzzy for a moment at the hint of such a fantasy. Affinity had acquired Kurt from the same underground fighting league as Knox. In the world of testosterone-filled naughty deliciousness, Kerry was standing between two of the finest examples of manhood. Opposite sides of the realm, of course, since Rhys was every bit as clean cut as Kurt was a bad boy, but oh what a ride it would be. Clearing her throat, she did her best to remember her part.

Reaching behind her, she tugged Rhys forward. "Kurt Travis, this is Rhys Collier. He will be my guest for the evening."

If Kurt's eyebrows weren't hidden beneath the shaggy blond hair hanging in his eyes, Kerry would have sworn they touched his hairline at the name. She bit back a smile as he eyed Rhys carefully. The two men shook hands. Rhys dipped his chin in acknowledgment.

"Lucky, lucky girl," Kurt murmured before snapping back to attention and getting down to business. "Welcome to club Affinity." He waved his security pass in front of the coded keypad beside him. The lock on the nondescript door disengaged. Swinging it wide, Kurt waved them inside. "Please enjoy your visit."

Walking backward through the

open doorway, Kerry towed Rhys inside. With her gaze locked on Rhys, she aimed her words at Kurt. "Don't you worry. We'll have a great time."

Rhys' mouth lifted in one corner and she realized he hadn't said a single word throughout the entire encounter. "Tell Kurt thank you, Rhys."

"Thank you, Rhys," he repeated obediently.

Kurt threw his head back, roaring with laughter. "Mistress Kerry, you have your hands full with this one."

She could still hear Kurt chuckling even after the door closed behind them, but she couldn't tear her eyes away from Rhys' face. A dimple appeared in one of his cheeks while he mouthed the word "mistress" with a question to it. His eyes darkened.

"Watch your step," she warned,

turning away from the temptation he presented. Once they turned the corner, a set of stairs led straight down into the huge underground club. Sultry music drifted up to meet them halfway through their descent. The temperature dropped. Chill bumps rose on her skin even while Kerry's body heat rose. It took every ounce of her willpower to keep from glancing over at Rhys to see his reaction when the first low moan reached their ears. Sheer lace curtains hanging from the ceiling fell all the way to the floor. They danced in time with the air blowing out of the vents. It gave the illusion of privacy while doing nothing to hide every fantasy from view. Even with the low lighting, they could see the acts taking place in the rooms separated by nothing more than translucent bits of lace. Fire danced along Kerry's skin. Excitement pounded through her.

Rhys' hand trailed down her back, brushing lightly over the curve of her ass before disappearing again. Kerry's nerve endings sang at the contact. Pausing mid-step, she drew him closer and motioned toward one of the fantasies taking place nearby. Stripped bare, a dark-haired woman covered in sweat strained against the mattress beneath her. Her hips lifted to meet the eager mouth of the blonde female settled between her legs. A man knelt near her head avidly watching the pair as he fucked her mouth. The sound of his moans matched perfectly in time with each hollowing of her cheeks.

"I wonder which she prefers," Kerry mused quietly enough so Rhys was forced to lean down to hear. A low chuckle fell from his lips as Rhys pressed his mouth to her ear.

"Definitely the woman," he said. She could hear the laughter in his voice as he added. "She's probably only half-aware of what she's doing to him."

"Agreed," Kerry said breathlessly. Her pussy clenched when Rhys didn't move away. The air leaving his lips brushed over the column of her neck, nearly causing her to pant. She needed relief. His hand closed over her hip holding her in place. She bit back a moan at the contact.

"Although I'm in no way conceding," he said, sinking his teeth lightly into her lobe before releasing it. "I will admit, I never took you for a fetish club kind of girl."

"I'm full of surprises."

She tried again to step away. He halted her motion. Nodding toward a different room, he asked, "Is that what I can expect from you? It does seem your style."

Kerry snuck a peek at the man wearing a mask and ball gag. His hands chained to a hook above his head. Even from their vantage point, she could see the way his dick twitched in anticipation of the crop landing across his bare ass.

Turning her head, she caught and held Rhys' stare. "Your night will be ten times better than his as long as you're still willing to submit."

His gaze dropped to her mouth for a moment. She wondered if he would kiss her. More importantly, she questioned if she would let him. After a few heartbeats, he released her and stepped away.

"I'm willing," he agreed. Her heart slammed against her chest. The idea of a submissive Rhys made her knees weaken. Forcing her feet to move, she stared straight ahead and focused on her goal.

"Come with me, then. Our little fantasy cove is just ahead." Kerry knew without looking that he did as she instructed. Turning to her left, she pushed aside a darker set of curtains, revealing an opulent king-sized bed draped in dark covers. A six-foot tall man stood proudly in his nudity at its edge. With his hands clasped behind his back, every line of his defined muscles stood out for her visual enjoyment. Kerry kicked out of her shoes. Meeting the man's light blue gaze, an understanding passed between them. This room offered more privacy than the others did. It had been a purposeful move on Kerry's part. Heavy drapery separated the space from the rooms surrounding them, blocking them from sight, while still allowing the sounds of pleasure around them to seep through.

She could feel Rhys' overwhelming presence at her back. Turning, she focused on him. "Rhys Collier, let me introduce Asher D'Ettore. He is a friend of mine." She watched Rhys' face for any hint of revulsion or surprise over the nude male waiting for them. Asher's golden skin and toned physique appealed to everyone, whether they wanted him sexually or not. With his jet-black hair and light-blue eyes, his beauty was almost beyond compare, but inside, Asher was easily the most exquisite person she'd ever known. The thought of Asher and Rhys together almost made her knees give out. They were the epitome of perfection.

"Nice to meet you, Asher," Rhys said politely. Kerry stamped down the happy dance growing inside of her. He wasn't rejecting anything outright.

Asher dipped his chin in

acknowledgment. His gaze never left Rhys. "Ciao, Rhys." Without giving Rhys time to object, she handed him the first order. "Strip."

The hunger in his eyes caused her panties to dampen and cling to her skin. His abs flexed as he tugged his shirt up and over his head. Her eyes locked on his sternum. The deep valley between the flat pads of his chest reminded her of his strength. His eyes never left her as he slipped his belt loose. The button worked loose on his jeans between his fingers. The idea of controlling so much suppressed alpha male caused her heart to race in anticipation.

The low music mixed with cries of pleasure thrummed throughout the room, beating like a pulse. Even with the sounds drowning out everything, she still heard his zipper sliding down. Her fingers clenched. She wanted to stroke him. The material parted, revealing his erection. Her mouth watered. Asher's hands settled on her hips from behind. The barely restrained desire pounding through her veins left her nerves raw. The sensation of satin slithering down her shoulders as Asher loosened her dress, combined with the vision of a now nude Rhys, made her moan. Rhys' eyes darkened.

"Come here." At her command, he closed the distance between them. Her clothes fell away under Asher's touch. Asher pressed his lips to her ear, speaking low enough for only her to hear.

"He's magnificent." She couldn't agree more.

Even though she knew Rhys wouldn't back down, she felt moved to offer him a way out. "If there is anything you are not willing to do, then you should say so now. There is no going back from this point. I won't take mercy on you."

A smirk twisted his lips. "I don't expect any."

Kerry reached behind her and Asher pressed a foil package along with a tube of liquid into her hands before moving away. He circled behind Rhys, running his fingers along his shoulders as he went. Rhys' nostrils flared. His eyelids swept downward, hiding his thoughts. A flush appeared across his cheekbones. His lips parted on a breath. The reaction told her more than words ever could.

"Tell me what you want," she demanded. "Everything."

Her channel pulsed. Fluid rolled down the inside of her thigh. Asher met her gaze over Rhys' shoulder. At her subtle nod, he touched his lips to Rhys' shoulder. The sight was so erotic she ripped open the condom to busy her hands. She wanted to stroke her clit and relieve some of the pressure building there. Rhys let out a sharp hiss when she rolled the condom down his shaft. The sound became a low moan when she squeezed cool liquid over him. She coated the entire sheath.

"I have a confession," she admitted as she watched his erection slipping through her oiled fingers. "I'm a bit of a voyeur." His dick twitched at the statement. A sinister smile pulled at the corners of her mouth. In that moment, she knew the truth. She'd been right about him.

*

Rhys had known, of course. The moment they entered the room and he set eyes on Asher, he'd been expecting this. It was almost funny. Rhys was sexual by nature. He'd never made any secret of his escapades. Most everyone who knew him knew he'd dated a couple of men in the past. He should've been surprised Kerry knew this tidbit, but he wasn't. Kerry possessed an uncanny ability to read people. The only real question was; did Kerry hope he would back down in the face of her challenge or did she want him to give in? Her expression gave nothing away. It didn't matter. He couldn't hide his body's reaction to the man standing at his back. His cock hadn't stopped twitching since they'd arrived. At this rate, he would explode before he saw any real action.

"Don't disappoint me."

Blood rushed in his ears at her command. "Not gonna happen."

The moment the assertion left his lips, Asher tugged his head back and covered Rhys' mouth with his. The familiar flavor of turned-on male exploded across

Rhys' taste buds at the first brush of Asher's tongue. Twisting in his arms, their teeth bumped. Their erections pressed between them. Gripping Asher's ass, Rhys hauled him closer, creating a delicious friction between them. It wasn't enough. Hot pre-cum spread across his abs, proving Asher enjoyed the rough treatment. Rhys didn't know any other way. Heaviness in his balls grew as desire gnawed at the base of his spine. Everything going on around them fell away. Nothing mattered except Rhys' yearning to bury his dick inside the man. Asher made a sound at the back of his throat. The need to possess him welled inside Rhys at the vibration of it around his tongue. Taking a step forward, he left Asher little choice except to step backward until he hit the edge of the mattress. Tearing his mouth away, Rhys caught the final wisp of Kerry's hair billowing out behind her as she slipped outside past the curtain. He didn't care. Strong fingers clasped his hips, pulling his attention back to the sexy man in his arms.

"What do you get out of this?" Rhys didn't know why he'd asked the question. He wasn't stopping.

"The same as you, I imagine."

Damn, that accent. It hit him in the gut. He stroked Asher's cock. "You can say no." A sinful expression crossed Asher's face. His lips drew Rhys' gaze. The bottom one was fuller than the top. Rhys wanted to taste it.

"I'm allowed to say no, am I? Peccato. You cannot."

A surprised chuckle escaped Rhys. Asher leaned in, swallowing the sound. Rhys crowded his space until he had him on his back. Their lips clashed, hard and hot. His needy cock twitching between them wouldn't wait. Lifting his head, Rhys searched for what he needed. Finding a pillow, he snagged it.

"Lift up." The words sounded wrecked, even to him.

At Rhys' urging, Asher's hips rose from the mattress enough for Rhys to shove the pillow under the small of his back. His heartbeat quickened. Trailing his fingers down Asher's thigh, he hooked Asher's leg over his hip. Pupils dilated, lips parted, Asher looked every bit as aroused as Rhys felt. His knuckles scraped along the inside of Asher's thigh as Rhys took himself in hand. Probing, Rhys slipped inside Asher's ass an inch, withdrawing again. Asher's erection jerked. He wanted this. Rhys could see it.

"Stroke yourself," Rhys demanded.

Reaching between their bodies,

Asher did as commanded. The moment his gorgeous blue eyes fell closed on a pant, Rhys surged forward burying himself inside Asher. He tried to hold still.

"Damn." The deep, silky and heavily accented curse broke past Asher's lips. "More."

It was all the permission Rhys needed. Rocking against him, Rhys followed the cues of the strangled cries leaving Asher's throat. Sweat beaded at the base of Rhys' spine. He wanted Asher's orgasm. Craved it. He couldn't look away from his face. Pressure built, drawing his balls up tight. Hot cum hit his stomach as a groan fell from Asher's lips. Rhys slammed his mouth down on Asher's, needing to taste the sounds coming from his deep inside his chest. Blood pounded in his ears. Flames licked at his skin. The tightness pulling at his dick was too much. The jet of semen shooting from the head of his cock brought a wave of ecstasy that stole the oxygen from his lungs.

Rhys spent a moment simply breathing in the scent of Asher's cologne before grasping the top of the condom and rolling away. Spotting a trashcan beside the bed, he swore as he got rid of the evidence.

"Thank fuck. I didn't have the strength to hunt a trashcan down."

A deep chuckle rumbled from Asher's side of the mattress, but he didn't comment. Exhaustion threatened to pull Rhys under. The awareness of his surroundings kept sleep at bay. As if the feeling were mutual, Asher scrubbed his hand over his face. With a groan, Asher's wonderful accent cut through the haze coating Rhys' mind. "I have to be at the office by six a.m. tomorrow. I suppose I must leave here."

"Yeah," Rhys agreed, unsure of what to say.

Asher moved to roll off the bed. In a flash of motion, Rhys found himself hovering over the man and pressing him back against the mattress.

"It mattered, okay?"

He couldn't explain why he needed Asher to know the night had not been pointless, but he did.

Asher's face and voice were devoid of emotion. "Okay."

It was a mask. Rhys didn't know why he wore it, but he recognized the defense mechanism for what it was. Lowering his head, Rhys touched his lips gently to Asher's, almost expecting a denial. The tip of his tongue teased open Asher's mouth. The way he tasted and smelled made Rhys incapable of allowing

Asher to leave without a final kiss goodbye. Maybe the sexy male would never think of him again. Even if he didn't, it hadn't been meaningless.

* * * * *

The moment Rhys turned his attention on Asher, Kerry slipped away. With her clothes left behind her, she traversed the maze-like hallways with the familiarity brought about by hundreds of nightly visits. Her body hummed. Even the brush of cool air against her thighs heightened her desire. When the unmarked door came into view, a shiver of excitement ran through her. Kerry's knuckles barely grazed the wood surface before it swung wide, revealing the man on the other side. A pair of worn jeans slung low on his hips. IIis broad shoulders and flat stomach were bare. She enjoyed the vision of golden skin. Blue eyes dropped to her painted toenails before slowly lifting to her face. They darkened, showing his lust even as his expression revealed nothing.

"I've been waiting."

"You're a patient man."

"No," Dane argued. "I'm not."

His hand shot out. Cold metal hit her wrist. Kerry didn't need to look. The familiar sensation of steel handcuffs sliding across her skin told her everything. With a tug, he hauled her inside, slamming the door shut behind her.

"You look delicious. Good enough to eat, in fact." The low tremble of his voice caressed her skin. Her hard nipples somehow managed to tighten further. "Have you enjoyed having all the power tonight?" She didn't answer. No good could come of anything she said. "I think it's time I took control, don't you?"

Kerry held her silence awaiting his

command. She didn't have to wait for long. "Get on the desk," Dane demanded as he crowded her against it. Meekly she obeyed. The cool planks almost shocked her system as they touched her inflamed flesh. Her juices soaked the surface as she slid backward. "On your back," he added when she didn't move quickly enough. With the ceiling staring down at her, Dane tugged her hands over her head, weaving the empty cuff through a metal bar on the wall before securing her other wrist. He eyed her nude body. Hunger etched in his face. Spreading her knees wide, he ran his finger down her slit. Her hips left the desk seeking his touch.

"Look how wet you are." She was powerless to do anything other than feel. "All of this for my little brother." Kerry didn't miss his emphasis on the word little. "I had a blindfold all picked out for you, but now, I think I should let you see who owns your pleasure." Gripping her thighs, he massaged her muscles, moving closer to her center with each pass. When he finally reached her cunt, his thumb dipped inside her opening. "Who owns this?"

She recognized he was punishing her. She took it as her due. "You do," she answered through parched lips. His touch eased and his face lost its hard edge at her confession. Using her moisture against her, he trailed a path from her channel to her asshole.

Without looking away from her face, he circled the puckered strawberry. "Tell me what you want," he demanded.

She didn't hesitate. "I want you to crawl up my body so I can taste your cock."

His eyes flared at her answer and

his hands went to work on his jeans. In a matter of moments, they were gone, and he was straddling her body. Only, instead of giving her what she wanted, he pressed his lips to hers. The tip of his tongue touched the corner of her mouth. She accepted him inside. Dane's familiar flavor coated her taste buds. It tasted like love and acceptance. Her body cradled his when he shifted positions. Dane's hard shaft ground against her needy pussy. Every word he spoke had been the truth. He did own her, but she owned him, as well. Just as she would never allow anyone to touch her the way he did, no one else tasted what belonged to her. The lifestyle surrounding them didn't matter in the least. She would kill any woman who encroached on her territory. There also wasn't a doubt in her mind that Dane would tear apart any man who attempted to steal her.

Taking hold of what control she could, Kerry sucked hard on his tongue while hooking her ankles at the small of his back in an attempt to draw him closer. Dane growled against her mouth. The blunt head of his cock probed at her entrance before easing away again. She whimpered, protesting the loss. Turning his head, Dane buried his face in the crook of her neck. He chuckled. The sound made her blood boil. Fury raced to the surface.

"Fuck me."

At her demand, he tsked. "You're so greedy."

He was right. When it came to him, she could not get enough. "Only for you."

At the admission, Dane surged forward, spearing her with his shaft. She cried out in surprise and pleasure. Buried to the hilt, Dane held still, giving her time to adjust to his intrusion. Going up on his elbow, he brushed her hair away from her face as he held her stare. The light above his head shimmered off the golden strands in his hair. He was such an enigma, a bad boy hidden behind the face of an angel.

"Thank you for helping my brother."

Her eyes fell closed at his words. She'd been so scared. He would never know how goddamn frightened she'd been of failing him. If Rhys couldn't find his way back home, she didn't know what it would eventually do to Dane. A tear slipped from the corner of her eye without her permission. Swallowing down her fear, she met his gaze again, attempting to make him see the truth.

"There is nothing I wouldn't do for you."

"This time, it wasn't for me."

"Everything is always for you," she

stressed but his face only softened further as he rocked his hips against her. Her clit pulsed at the direct contact. Dipping his head, Dane froze an inch from her mouth. He ground his pelvis against her again making her pant.

"You couldn't stand the sight of his pain," he whispered. "It's one of the many reasons I love you so fucking much it hurts." Without giving her another chance to argue, he sealed his mouth over hers. Her reasons no longer mattered when he was pumping inside her. Kerry's mind couldn't cling to anything other than the pressure building between her legs. The tingle continued to grow with each pull of his skin across her love button. Her greedy cunt convulsed and sucked the seed from his dick. Even focused on her goal, she didn't miss the words he whispered as she came apart. "You are my whole goddamn world."

Chapter Three

"What the hell? Do you work here or something? Every time I stop by, you're here."

Screwing up his face, Dane scoffed at Rhys' question. "No."

"Okay," Rhys drawled.

"Why are you here?" Dane asked before Rhys could question him further.

"I came for Kerry. She owes me something."

Dane bit the inside of his cheek to keep from smiling or growling. He wasn't sure yet which side he would emerge on. Either way, he didn't want to take any chances of giving himself away. When he didn't offer up her whereabouts, Rhys rocked back on his heels and his eyebrows rose in question.

"Well, I guess I'll just check inside for Kerry then…"

Dane shrugged. "Knock yourself out. Like I said, I don't work here."

Rhys shook his head as he turned away. Dane fought the urge to pound his head on the countertop. As the door swept closed behind his brother, Dane shifted his gaze to where Kerry sat on the floor at his feet.

"You won't be able to hide from him forever."

She blew her bangs away from her face. "I know. I don't intend to, so don't worry. I have a plan."

"Does this plan include sleeping with my little brother?"

With a roll of her eyes, she punched him in the thigh. "Of course not! You ought to know by now I'm a lot of things, but I'm not a cheat."

Lowering his lids, he swept a hot gaze over the body he could not get enough of, and his balls grew heavy. Her nipples showed through her shirt, proving her body's willingness to participate in whatever he planned. He could hear the lust in his voice when he responded. "I know you're not a cheat. There aren't enough hours in your day for anyone except for me. As for you being many things, you are really only one thing. Mine."

Out of the corner of his eye, he saw the front door swing open but Dane couldn't look away from Kerry. Her expression gave him every reassurance a man could need. She loved him. He knew it with only a glance.

"You're always here," a deep Italian accent rumbled from across the counter.

Kerry jumped, visibly startled by the

sound. Dane loved that he was able to hold her attention so completely with only a stare. Dane still didn't look away from her as he responded.

"I'm hearing that a lot today."

Kerry stood, making herself known. Asher smiled knowingly at them both. "Ah, now I understand your inability to stay away. We should all be as lucky." It was obvious what Asher thought Kerry had been doing on the floor. Dane bit back a grin when she didn't try to disabuse Asher's suspicions. Instead, he leaned on the counter as she attempted to move Asher along.

"Yes. Well, you should head in then. Don't you think?" She let the question hang in the air between them. Asher's grin turned shrewd.

"I do believe I'm intruding. Far be it for my usual daily workout to interfere with your..." he paused, eyeing them both carefully before continuing, "time together," he finished with a wink.

Striding away, Asher didn't give them time to argue before disappearing inside the club. "Huh. His usual daily workout. I see your plan," Dane said the moment they were alone.

Kerry's eyes skirted away. "I have no idea what you mean."

Guilty. "Uh-huh." Dane straightened to his full height and shoved his hands in his pockets to keep from reaching for her. In his mind, he was burying his fingers in her hair, pulling gently at the locks as he hauled her body against his. He knew exactly how she tasted, the sounds she made and how hot her cunt got while squeezing his cock. Damn, she was like oxygen to him, completely necessary.

Rhys checked every unlocked room except for the women's locker room before finally giving it up as a bad job. Unable to find Kerry anywhere inside, Rhys headed back toward the door. He wondered for the hundredth time if she'd wussed out on him. The overwhelming sense of someone watching him crawled up his back. Scanning the room once more, Rhys spotted a familiar form striding toward the locker rooms. His every nerve ending went on high alert. In a single glance, he was every bit as turned on as he'd been the night before when the sexy male's body had been pressed against his. A set of light blue eyes met his before skirting away. There was not even a hint of recognition crossing Asher's face before dismissing him. It hurt more than expected. No strings. The reminder did nothing to ease the tightening of the muscles in his chest. Damn. The ten-thousand-dollar business suit threw him off-balance. He should have known. The cultured accent, expensive cologne, and mannerisms all spoke of a certain lifestyle. Yep. Out of his league. Whatever. It wasn't important. Fuck. Going for the exit, he caught a glimpse of Kerry and Dane in the foyer. Something about the way they looked at each other gave him pause. Instead of charging out the glass door, he hung back for a minute.

Kerry snagged the front of Dane's t-shirt and tugged him forward. He kept his hands shoved deep in his pockets, but he went willingly. Since he stood almost a foot taller than her, Dane was forced to lean down to touch his forehead to hers. An inch away from one another, they kept their gazes locked. Neither appeared to speak nor did they touch each other in any other way.

It wasn't possible. There was no way this could happen twice in one lifetime. Both of his brothers loved a woman who had shared some form of sexual experience with him. Kerry had plans to do it again. There was no goddamn way. He couldn't deny the truth staring him in the face. They loved each other. The fucking bitch. Anger like he'd not experienced in a long time came rushing to the surface. The door banged against the wall before he recognized he'd been the one who threw it open. Kerry and Dane stared at him as if he was insane. No doubt, he looked it at the moment. Dane was better now. He was finally recovering from his addictions, and she would destroy him.

"Are you fucking kidding me?"

"Look, man, I can explain."

Dane's attempt to soothe his temper brought Rhys up short. "You have nothing to explain. You're not the one screwing around."

Damned if they didn't both look guilty, and for once, Kerry had nothing to say. Her lack of argument left him off-kilter. The couple exchanged glances. His head hurt. Something wasn't right, and as usual, he was the only one who didn't understand what was going on. Kerry dropped her chin and stared at the toes of her shoes. Dane seemed...unfazed. Scrubbing his hands across his forehead, Rhys did his best to call his temper under control. The cool look on Asher's face floated across his mind.

"You know what? I don't want to know." Stepping around Dane, he headed out the front entrance and straight for his truck. He shouldn't have come back to this town. His steps slowed when his car and the man waiting beside it came into view. How had he beaten him outside without walking right past him? His tie was missing. The blue shirt that matched his eyes perfectly, was unbuttoned at the collar leaving a hint of olive skin showing. Rhys could almost smell him. It did nothing to help his black mood.

The moment he spotted Rhys, Asher straightened away from the vehicle. "I wasn't ignoring you." His eyes weren't cool any longer. Rhys struck without thought, crowding him against the door of his truck. He didn't give a shit who was watching as he flattened his palms against the sun-warmed steel on either side of Asher.

"I know you're not."

The wave of raw lust rolling off

Asher's body punched him in the gut. "I didn't wish to embarrass you by openly acknowledging you. Now, I see you're not bothered."

"Really?" Rhys could hear the sarcastic note in his voice, but his temper wouldn't allow him to stop. He ran his gaze over Asher's expensive clothing. "I got the impression you were merely slumming it with me. Perhaps you're the one who is embarrassed."

Asher's entire demeanor changed in an instant at the accusation. "Ah. I see." He stepped out of his hold, leaving Rhys no choice except to let him go, or physically restrain him. Rhys watched him walking away. The confidence in Asher's stride held Rhys' attention much longer than it should.

Before Asher could get too far away to fix things, Rhys spoke up, stopping him.

"I'm sorry."

In a flash, Asher managed to reverse their roles. The solid door came against Rhys' back as the pissed-off man went nose to nose with him. "Do you know what your problem is?" Without waiting for an answer, Asher added, "You're obviously used to dealing with people who are weak, and I am anything but. I happen to know my worth. If you ever figure out yours then you know where to find me."

Pushing away from the truck, he left Rhys alone and speechless. Not to mention, his dick was now hard as a rock. Holy hell. The smell of Asher's cologne hung in the air. The accent, damn, he'd forgotten what the sound of it did to him. With a curse, he pushed away from the truck. There wasn't any sense in staying here any longer. The moment the door closed behind him, he froze. How had

98

Asher known which vehicle belonged to him? It was one question he might not ever get an answer to since it seemed he'd fucked everything up.

* * * * *

The third beer and cool night air did much to calm him. Nothing compared to the Vegas skyline. The bedroom he occupied at Knox's place had one hell of a view from its balcony. Millions of tiny lights in the distance reminded Rhys of how small he was in comparison. Kicking his feet up onto the railing, he settled deeper into his chair. When the French doors opened and Dane strolled out, he wasn't the least bit surprised. His brother had always been a sneaky bastard. Rhys tipped back the longneck, doing his best to ignore Dane as he claimed the empty chair next to him.

Fishing around in the cooler at his feet, Dane came out with a bottle of water.

"A lot has changed around here since you left," he said as he twisted the lid off.

"You could have fooled me. This shit is feeling real familiar."

Dane chuckled. "You've always been good at turning a blind eye to things."

"In other words, I'm a self-absorbed ass. Thanks," Rhys added with a wince.

"No. I've never believed that, because you can be wonderfully observant when something piques your interest."

Rhys threw up a hand. "Great. Now, I'm a self-absorbed ass with A.D.D."

With an exasperated sigh, Dane shook his head. "You're full of heart. Unfortunately, you were also raised in the same home I was. You've learned to protect your heart from things you know will hurt. Growing up, you never wanted to see Knox as a victim, or even as human for that matter. As a result, you wrapped yourself in your anger when he left us behind. However, I remember those days all too well. Actually, I'm a bit surprised he made it long enough to ditch us, not that it mattered in the end. He was still just as haunted after he left. Of course, you were too young to hear about the multiple suicide attempts."

That got Rhys' attention. "Who? Knox?"

Ignoring the disbelief in his tone, Dane simply nodded. "It was bad." A thoughtful look passed over his face. "Honestly, it was a bit of a relief when he finally shut down."

"Damn," Rhys breathed unsure of what to think. "I knew he owned a massive death wish, but I had no idea."

Dane looked away and took a deep pull on his water bottle. With his eyes glued to some point in the distance, he finally spoke. "You had no clue about a lot of things."

With a helpless gesture, Rhys did his best to grapple with the way Dane's voice had gone flat. "I don't understand. I mean, I realize Dad had his problems. We might have been starved for affection, but he never laid a finger on us." Not that he needed to, Rhys silently conceded. The emotional abuse they'd suffered daily was enough to fell a full-grown man.

Dane let out a mirthless laugh as soon as the words left Rhys' mouth. "He never laid a finger on you, because he knew we would kill him. We took it on the chin, and he left you alone almost as if we had a silent agreement. Knox was too passionate to keep his head down. He was always half an inch away from having it knocked from his shoulders. It's no wonder he can take a damn beating better

102

than any man alive. He's had a ton of practice. Of course, then there was me." He paused, and since Rhys was watching his profile, he caught a glimpse of the sardonic smile passing briefly over his features before disappearing. "I was the constant reminder of mom's infidelity."

Rhys' mouth fell open. Never in memory had someone caused him such a level of disbelief. "What?"

Dane flashed him a mocking grin before looking away. "Come on, Rhys. You seriously have never questioned why I am the only blond-haired, blue-eyed member of an otherwise dark-haired family? I don't look anything like any of you."

He didn't, but genetics were crazy sometimes. "So what? Blond hair doesn't mean you're not our father's son."

"I'm sorry but it's true."

Rhys didn't know what to say. It

explained so much. He didn't want to accept it. Dane didn't wait for him to dredge up some half-ass response. "Things have changed for everyone since his death. It was almost as if he was a black cloud suffocating us. Of course, Mandy is truly the one who set Knox free. He needs her, you know?"

Thankful for something else to cling to, Rhys grasped hold of the topic. "Yes. I do. They both needed me to leave to move forward with their lives. Maybe I looked like a dick for pulling up stakes without a word. It wasn't a good idea for me to stay."

Dane nodded absently and tipped back his water again. "I should have stayed for you, though," Rhys admitted.

"No." Dane's one word came out with enough bitterness dripping from it that Rhys was taken aback. He'd never heard Dane sound so hardened. When he looked over at him, he almost looked like Knox for a moment. There was a family resemblance, after all. "There comes a time when you need to man-up, Rhys. I was a mess, and I want your word you'll never clean up after me again. Hopefully, there will never come a time where I'll have to call this promise in. Nonetheless, I want you to swear to me you won't."

His heart sank. "Don't ask this of me, please? You're my brother."

Dane nodded. "And I always will be, but you have to let me sink or swim all on my own."

"But this thing with Kerry," Rhys argued. To his surprise, Dane threw his head back and roared with laughter before he could finish voicing his concern. "I'm not finding any of this particularly funny," Rhys grumbled.

"Dude," Dane said, turning shining

eyes his way. "Kerry is my wife."

"What? You've got to be joking? There's no way. It's not possible. Fuck! I've had some form of sexual contact with both of my brother's wives."

"You slept with Mandy?"

Rhys groaned at the question as he recognized his mistake. "Let's focus on one thing at a time."

Dane released a low whistle. "I can't believe you're still breathing if you touched Mandy."

Cutting his eyes at Dane, he gave in. "It was before they got together."

"Still," Dane said with a shrug. "Knox is not exactly known for his reasonable thinking."

Dragging them back on topic, Rhys felt moved to point out the obvious. "Yet you don't seem the least bit upset about Kerry."

"I think it's time you accept something."

"Really? What else could I possibly need to deal with tonight? It's been pretty enlightening already."

"This family is filled with sexual deviants." In spite of the situation, Rhys barked out a laugh at Dane's answer. His brother looked almost embarrassed as he added. "So, um, you know the club where you met Kerry last night?"

"As if I could forget?"

"Hmm, well, I sort of own it."

Rhys almost fell out of his chair. "Shut the fuck up. You do not." He could not see his brother as the owner of a fetish club. "I have to know." Even to his ears, Rhys sounded exactly like a twelve-year-old girl digging for gossip. He didn't care.

"I was kind of numb for a little while after rehab and Jimmy came to me with an offer."

"Jimmy? Knox's trainer? That Jimmy?"

"Yep."

"You know, I'm not surprised."

"Anyhow," Dane continued as if Rhys had not interrupted him. "It was a bit of a side business for him, but he'd met some blonde chick half his age. She'd agreed to marry him so he needed to dump it fast before she found out about it."

"Wait," Rhys said holding up a hand. "Is this girl's name Peggy?"

"Um, it's Penny actually."

"That old bastard," Rhys cursed under his breath.

"As I was saying," Dane pressed on. "Even though I wasn't in a good place, Max loaned me the money and I bought it."

"So Max knows about this place too?"

"Yeah. Ryan and he are members."

Rhys shook his head in wonder. "I can't believe this."

Dane nodded. "Those two are some freaky dudes."

The memory of witnessing Max on his knees floated across Rhys' mind. "Seems like I heard that somewhere already, but Kerry?" He didn't bother hiding his skepticism.

"Yeah. I was a bit surprised, too, the first time I saw her there. Actually, the look on her face when she saw me was priceless." He fell silent. A smile touched his lips as if he could still picture it.

"I'm happy for you, I think, but I wish someone would have said something. I didn't want this. Letting go of Mandy was one of the hardest things I've ever done. I know no one believes I love her, but I do. The idea of her spending the rest of her life with Knox," he shook his head unable to truly express what the knowledge did to him. "If it was anyone else, I would still be on her doorstep doing my best to win her back. Fuck whomever she married. Except, it's my brother, which changes everything. Now, I got this shit with Kerry on my conscience too."

Dane crossed his arms over his chest appearing thoughtful for a minute. When he finally spoke, it came out haltingly as if he chose his words with care. "Unlike everyone else, I know you love Mandy. You have since you were sixteen so it's not likely to change anytime soon. The thing is, she needs something different out of life than you do, and I think—deep down—you've always known it. Knox and her, they both crave an ordinary life. You can't give it to her because no matter how hard you try,

110

you're not normal."

"Tomorrow, I'll look back on this conversation and count how many times I was insulted."

A line appeared between Dane's brows. "Why? There's nothing wrong with being different. I understand your feelings about Kerry, but she did try to warn you. You're not kinky enough for her."

Rhys groaned. Damn. Was there no detail Dane did not know?

Dane laughed at his reaction. "Think of the experience as matchmaking. Kerry knew you would be perfect for Asher and she was right. Not to mention, what do you have to feel guilty about anyhow? You saw her naked." He shrugged. "So? Who cares? She is fucking gorgeous as hell. I get to brag about her being mine. Do you feel bad she touched your dick? Dude. I'd like to know who hasn't." Rhys let out a loud grunt and dropped his head against the back of the chair. The motion only caused Dane to laugh again as he added, "There will never be more between the two of you than last night. Some smoking hot shit goes down inside my club, but Kerry doesn't share anyone's bed except mine. I'm the same with her. Let it go. You have nothing to be ashamed of."

Damned if he couldn't hear how much Dane loved Kerry in every word he spoke about her. "I can't believe you married Kerry."

"Yet you were more than willing to fuck her at the first opportunity."

Rhys shook his head in defeat. His tone came out sounding every bit as childish as he felt. "She's so evil."

Pride filled Dane's voice when he spoke. "Yep. She's amazing. I'm not a bit ashamed to admit I traded one addiction for another. I can't get enough."

"Lucky bastard. I hate everyone."

"Kerry seemed to think you hit things off with Asher."

Rhys pulled a face as he admitted, "I did what I always do, fucked things up. Not that it matters since I have no idea how to get in touch with him again or anything."

"Sounds to me as if you like him."

Rhys didn't miss the hint of hope laced in the statement. A picture of the flush of arousal riding high on Asher's cheeks and his lips parting on a gasp as he came floated across Rhys' mind. "Yeah. I like him."

"Good thing you've got me then," Dane said, bringing Rhys' gaze his way. "He works out at Grid Iron at the same time every day. I imagine if you turn up there tomorrow around the time you did today, you'll trip right over him."

"The resemblance between you and Kerry is amazing right now."

Dane threw his head back, roaring with laughter at Rhys' comment. For the first time, Rhys realized his brother was healthy. More importantly, he had a brother again. "I've missed you," he admitted before realizing he would do so.

Dane sobered at the confession. "I missed you too, little brother. Don't go away again."

"You either," Rhys shot back.

With a somber nod, Dane agreed. "Deal. I do have to go home, though. Don't drink too much."

Rhys scoffed at the lecture while watching Dane slip back inside the house. Secretly, he'd never been more grateful to have someone scold him.

* * * * *

The shirt slipped over Dane's head, exposing his toned back. Kerry could tell he was trying to be quiet while fumbling around in the moonlit room. As usual, she'd been unable to fall asleep without him. She'd known the moment he'd snuck into their bedroom. While he pushed his jeans down his hips, she enjoyed the show. The tattooed words that scrolled down his spine, held her gaze. There wasn't enough moonlight streaming through the blinds to read them. It didn't matter. She knew them by heart.

"Weakness (noun) An irresistible object of desire. Strength (noun) A degree of intensity or valuable asset. You are my greatest strength and weakness."

She owned exactly seventeen handwritten copies of the same words. He'd written them to her in a letter, once a week, every week he'd been in rehab and then once more the day he'd asked her to marry him. They were her most treasured possession. When he sat on the edge of the bed, Kerry couldn't resist any longer. She flattened her palm against the words. Dane leaned into her touch.

"I thought you were sleeping."

She didn't bother saying anything since it was obvious she was not. Instead of climbing underneath the covers with her, Dane stared at the wall, turning inside himself. Sometimes he fell into black moods and she couldn't reach him. She hated it.

After a moment, Dane broke the silence. "I am the older brother. It should have been me taking care of him. Not the other way around."

"Neither of you are dead yet. It's not too late to start."

"He never gave up on me."

"I know."

He looked at her then. "How do I repay him?"

"By never allowing it to happen again," she answered. She'd never meant anything more in her life, but Dane glanced away.

"It's not enough." His words were so quiet she almost didn't hear them. With more force, he added, "Tell me this thing with Asher will work."

"It'll work," she answered immediately. "Asher is strong and proud. He'll bend Rhys to his will."

A smile passed over Dane's face. "Exactly what the cockiest of my brothers needs."

"You think he's the cockiest? I have to disagree."

Tilting his chin, Dane watched her through half-lidded eyes. "Really?" He drawled.

She nodded slowly. "You have him beat by a long shot."

Before she realized it would happen, Dane pounced and pinned her beneath him. Digging his fingers into her ribcage, he pulled a giggle from her lips.

"I'll show you cocky."

"I do love to see your cock," she teased between gasps for air.

Chapter Four

Drew Alexander, the US Heavyweight Champion and owner of No Rival, was one of the few people Rhys considered to be a friend. At least as much of a friend as anyone was to Drew. The huge, bald man didn't invite conversation, but the few times he'd confided in Rhys left him thinking highly of the elusive fighter. Even though Rhys had been undecided on whether he would return to Vegas, he'd continued paying his monthly dues to the exclusive training center during his absence. No Rival was part of his blood. His family. The familiar scent of leather, sweat, and testosterone let him know he'd done the right thing. The spongy floor, concrete walls and multicolored bags hanging from the ceiling sent a burst of nostalgia rolling through him. However, the sight of Drew attempting to correct one of the new fighters' stances while holding a blonde-haired baby in his arms, left Rhys feeling downright homesick.

The men crowding around the world's best MMA fighter hung on his every word. Their rapt attention showed they understood the privilege of learning from Drew.

"Some things never change," Rhys called out, interrupting them.

Drew tossed a grin in his direction as if he'd known Rhys was there all along. Most likely, he had. "And some things are always changing," Drew said. Then without warning, he handed the child off to Rhys.

The tiny girl, close to a year in age, with large gray eyes, looked every bit as surprised as Rhys felt. After a moment, she seemed to accept her situation. Wrapping one arm around his neck, she silently turned away to watch Drew. With his arms free, he moved between each of the students, making minor tweaks to each of their techniques. Only when they all had it down did he make his way back to Rhys.

"Thanks, man," he said, attempting to take repossession of his daughter. She was having none of it. A loud screech rent the air, piercing Rhys' eardrum. Her tiny fingernails dug into the back of Rhys' neck. Drew held his hands up showing his surrender. "What the hell was I thinking? Even miniature females find you irresistible."

With a giggle, Adalyn buried her head against Rhys' shoulder flashing her daddy an adorable smile.

"It's fine," Rhys said. "I was

planning on hanging out for a bit anyhow." He looked her over. The same four-tooth smile Adalyn had shown Drew came again at his inspection. "I can't believe how big you've gotten." She'd been a tiny baby when Rhys had left town.

"Time flies," Drew agreed, drawing his attention back to him. "I forgot for a second. I don't see you every day. Are you sure you're okay to hang onto her for a minute?"

"Yeah. I'm cool." He started to add a joke about handling females. The sure knowledge Drew would kill him was the only thing stopping him.

"Thank God. I've needed to take a piss for over an hour now." He eyed the men around them for a second, before adding, "I don't trust any of these dudes with my baby." Without waiting for Rhys to reassure him again, Drew disappeared.

"Daddy piss."

Rhys bit down on his bottom lip, hard. No matter how he tried, he couldn't stop the snort from escaping at Adalyn's words. "Your daddy is a bad influence."

She didn't seem to care. Popping her fingers in her mouth, Adalyn went back to resting her head against his chest. A few familiar faces ambled over, shaking hands and giving him updates before Drew reappeared.

"Sorry about that. I walked by the office and the damn phone was ringing off the hook."

"Damn phone."

Rhys couldn't hold back his silky chuckle this time at Adalyn's words. Drew's reaction didn't help the matter. Smacking himself across the forehead, he let out a loud groan. "I swear, dude. She only repeats the bad things I say. She has her mother's naughty sense of humor."

"Momma naughty."

Drew's gray eyes flipped up to the ceiling as if seeking help from a higher power.

"If it's any consolation, Aubree is the one at fault here. She's allowing you to keep your daughter in this place." Rhys shook his head, running down the list of rough men who trained there before adding, "Nothing good could come of that."

"I'm telling her you said so."

At Drew's threat, Rhys immediately shook his head. "Uh, no you're not."

A smile spread across Drew's face. "Oh yeah, I am."

In spite of knowing Aubree would be murdering him soon, Rhys felt lighter than he had in a long time. It was just like old times.

* * * * *

Asher drove a Jag. It was the F-TYPE, the most expensive one. Rhys should have known. After spending an hour catching up with Drew, he'd decided he would indeed head over to Grid Iron and trip right over Asher as Dane suggested. Crossing his arms over his chest and his feet at the ankles, Rhys leaned against the door of his F-150 as he waited for Asher to step out of his car. Asher wasn't in any hurry. Even though Rhys recognized the man's game, he took it as his due. He'd insulted him, and Asher was doing his best to make him pay. The aroma of Asher's cologne hit Rhys first. A part of Rhys worried he'd never get hard again without remembering the scent. The dark gray suit he wore looked sexy as hell. It only made Asher's eyes seem even lighter in coloration. Doing what he always did when he was nervous, Rhys fell back on his natural charm as Asher eyed him questioningly.

"Turns out it wasn't hard to figure out my worth once properly motivated."

Asher was trying not to smile. Rhys could see him biting it back. "Self-love is a good thing in moderation."

Although Rhys knew what he meant, he still snorted at his choice of terminology. "My grandmother said you'd go blind otherwise."

A low chuckle fell from his perfectly shaped lips. Rhys' gaze locked onto them. He wanted him. "My nonna says something similar."

Forcing himself to concentrate on their conversation, Rhys switched his attention back to Asher's eyes. It didn't help. "Where are you from originally?" The freaking accent was driving him insane. He never dreamed the sound of someone's voice could be such a turn-on.

Asher did not shift under his stare even though Rhys felt sure his every desire was etched in the details of his face. "Bolzona." After a moment, Asher clarified, "Italy."

"Have dinner with me."

"Italy makes you hungry?" Laughter sounded heavy in his voice. Rhys couldn't bring himself to smile.

He shook his head. "You make me hungry." Asher's lips parted in surprise. He'd not expected the open admission. Rhys could see it. Good. Rhys wanted him off-kilter. It was hard to hang onto control while attempting to hold onto balance. Asher glanced at the club's entrance and Rhys could feel his indecision. "Just dinner. That's all I'm asking for."

Asher's mouth turned up in one corner. He reached inside his jacket and pulled out a card and pen. Scratching out a set of numbers on the back, Asher handed it over. "If you know where Cal's Grill is, I suppose I could be ready by seven."

After scanning the phone number, Rhys tucked the card into the pocket of his jeans while doing his best to hide the triumph rushing through his veins. "Then that's what time I'll meet you there."

Asher dipped his chin in agreement. "I've given you the number to my mobile in case you change your mind. Otherwise, I'll see you at seven. Ciao."

Rhys watched him until he disappeared inside. Baby steps. He would take one tiny step at a time until Asher was left wondering when he'd been swept away.

* * * * *

Cal's Grill acted as neutral ground for

Asher. Quiet enough for conversation while too brightly lit for intimacy, it was the perfect location to get to know someone. The man sitting across from him intrigued him. Rhys Collier, while rough around the edges, seemed strangely vulnerable at times. Asher wanted to know more. Wide shoulders, perfectly angled face and sweet brown eyes were only a few of Rhys' many attributes.

Asher was rarely fascinated by anything. Rhys didn't fidget or chatter nervously. Everything about Rhys screamed cool confidence. Tilting his head back, Rhys' gaze moved over the restaurant décor. While he seemed absorbed by the gigantic bull's head hanging above the nearby bar, Asher couldn't look away from the skin peeking out at him from the open collar of Rhys' shirt. He'd tasted that exact spot. It had been delicious. He wanted to feel it against his tongue again. The air felt too thick. Rhys' gaze met his and Asher lifted his glass to his lips to hide his reactions to the man.

If Rhys guessed at his thoughts, he didn't show it. Instead, he chose to break the ice. "What do you do for a living?"

Thankful for a topic, Asher jumped on it. "I'm a solicitor."

"It's strangely fitting you should be an attorney."

Asher didn't know what Rhys' comment was supposed to mean. He let it go. "What about you?"

"I'm a professional fighter."

It took every ounce of self-control within Asher to keep from repeating Rhys' response. He wasn't a bit surprised to learn he used his physical strength against others for a living. Power needed an outlet. Rhys had it in droves.

"Pugilist?"

"It's a bit similar, I suppose," he agreed. Shaking his head, he added. "No, not really."

A surprised laugh slipped from Asher over his answer. "Which is it?"

"It's not. I'm an MMA fighter. It's a mixture of several fighting styles, such as Judo and Muay Thai. Basically, it's any combination deemed effective to win a match."

"Ah. I have heard of it. They do have a training center at Grid Iron for such a thing, but I did not sign up for the benefit. I can hardly appear in court with bruises covering my face. Do you enjoy this line of work?"

"If I say 'yes' does it make me sound violent?"

Did it? Asher hadn't thought about

it before asking the question. He was simply making conversation.

"I don't see why it would," he answered after a moment. "If you have worked hard toward this goal and are proud of your accomplishments, then you shouldn't care what I think."

Rhys nodded, appearing thoughtful. "I am proud. My father was Middleweight Champion. It has cast certain aspirations on all his sons."

"You, of course, have worked to prove you are a man of worth without his name, I'm sure."

A flash of surprise crossed Rhys' features before disappearing as quickly as it appeared. "Of course," he agreed. "Not many people realize it, though."

Asher imagined, when it came to Rhys, they didn't. "People will see as much or as little as you allow."

Rhys' lips turned up in one corner, while his gaze dropped to Asher's mouth. It was a ploy. Even as Asher recognized the move for the defense mechanism it was, he still wanted to drag Rhys to the floor.

"Are you saying I've exposed myself to you?"

Two could play at this game. Asher intentionally relaxed his pose, slipping down an inch in his chair. He raked Rhys' body with his gaze, making sure Rhys saw every ounce of desire he felt for the man.

"Yes. As I recall it, you did. It was delicious."

He waited until Rhys' eyes glazed over before snatching his heated look away. Returning to his earlier serious tone, Asher added, "But as it happens, I understand because my life has been similar to yours. My papa's services are much sought after in Bolzona. This career path was chosen for me before I was born. There was never a chance I would do anything else, and I exceeded all expectations. With one minor twist to the story, that is. After law school and two years of training at his firm, I passed Esame di Stato, um, it is Italy's equivalent of the bar exam. It allows me to practice law internationally. Someone else may have planned my life, but I did not want to give all of it away."

By the time he'd finished with his story, Rhys had sat forward with both elbows leaning on the table, seeming completely focused on Asher's every word. A luminous smile twisted his lips.

"I'm beyond curious to know how they reacted when you chose to practice here."

A chuckle slipped from Asher's lips. "It was priceless. My parents were horrified but could think of no argument against it. After all, I was doing as expected even if I wasn't. I know they wanted me to work at the family law firm, living my father's life exactly as he had. I could not do it."

A picture of the life he'd avoided played out across his mind. Asher suppressed a shudder. Damn, he'd avoided a nightmare. Dragging himself away from the place in his head, he focused on Rhys instead.

"What about you? What twist did you weave into your life's story to avoid a pre-written fate?"

Rhys, who had been taking a sip from his water glass, almost choked on his drink at the question. It took Asher a moment to realize he was snickering.

"I became the current middleweight champion."

Asher pressed his lips together attempting to hide his mirth. "There you go. No one can say you did not earn it now."

The food appeared and disappeared without any real notice. By the time the check came, Asher made an important discovery. He was completely at ease. They were equally matched on several levels. Their time together passed too quickly and Asher didn't want it to end. Unfortunately, as they stood to leave, Rhys' demeanor shifted. His voice and eyes became seductive. The charmer made an appearance. He knew Rhys' game and did not intend to play by his rules. It was a chess match. Advance and retreat. Asher was not immune, but he equally was not a simpleton. The Rhys he had met inside Affinity had been the genuine version. His desire had been real. Asher refused to settle for less. When Rhys brought arousal without manipulation, Asher would ruin him for all others, but until then...

"Spend the night with me."

Asher scoffed at the soft demand. "You said dinner and nothing more. I agreed. We've had dinner now it is time for the nothing-more stage."

Rhys' eyes shone with humor. "You're right. I did say as much. I wouldn't want to go back on my word."

The warm night air slapped Asher in the face. Pausing to inhale the heavy scent of summertime into his lungs, he barely restrained himself from tilting his head back to stare at the sky. Asher wasn't much of a dreamer. Since fantasizing had not been penciled into his schedule as a child, he'd not developed much of a taste for it. However, lately, he'd become dissatisfied with his lot. Not tonight. He knew the reason was standing so close to his side he could feel the heat from his skin. Shit.

"My car is over there," Asher said, with a nod in its direction. Best he moved along before he gave in.

"Can I, at the very least, walk you to your car?"

The pitfalls were minimal, he decided. "If you'd like." Then he made a mistake. He glanced over at Rhys.

"I would." Those two words sounded sexy as sin falling from Rhys' perfect lips. A shiver ran down Asher's spine. His feet moved toward his car before the rest of him could do something he'd regret. Rhys didn't exactly walk him to his vehicle. It was more he walked behind him to his car.

The moment they reached the door, Asher did his best to cut off anything further. "We are here, so this is good night."

Asher had one hand on the door and one foot inside when Rhys stopped him. "What are you doing Friday night?"

Asher slid behind the wheel while running through his schedule in his mind. "I'm due in court that morning, but I'm free from midafternoon on."

"Would you like to go see a fight with me? My older brother, Knox, has an underground match. It is unsanctioned so it's not exactly the same as what I do, but I'd love to take you to see it. Plus, you can meet my brother afterward."

Asher was quick to agree. The amount of pride Rhys had shown over his work made him curious to see it in action. "I'd love to."

Taking out the card Asher had given him earlier in the day, Rhys squatted down beside him. He dialed the number written on the back. Asher felt his phone buzz inside his pocket. "There. Now, you have my number too. Text your address to me and I'll pick you up at eight."

"Sounds good. I suppose I should say ciao."

Rhys made a move, as if to stand, but instead he continued forward until Asher found his head against the headrest. His mouth found Asher's. The darkened corner of the parking lot gave Asher the sense of seclusion in a crowd. Losing himself, he buried his fingers in Rhys' hair, tugging him closer. A clicking noise broke through the growing haze of lust. It took Asher a moment to realize Rhys had buckled his seat belt. Pulling away, Rhys cupped his cheek while holding his gaze.

"Be careful, and in case I forgot to say so, you look hot as hell tonight."

Without waiting for a response, Rhys closed the door. Asher watched him walk away, accepting the inevitable. He was totally fucked.

* * * * *

He made it exactly ten hours and eighteen minutes after their dinner date before giving in to temptation.

Thank you for dinner.

With the text sent, Asher spent five solid minutes staring at the face of his phone watching for any response. When it didn't come, he wanted to kick himself for being an idiot. It's not as if he hadn't known he wasn't anything more than a passing fancy. Best it ended now. By the time he made it home from work and settled in for the night, he'd almost convinced himself it was true. Every noise he heard, from the sound of his keys hitting the cherry wood table by the front door to his shower firing to life, shone a bright light on how empty his life had become. For years, he'd never noticed anything lacking. Lately, things had changed. With his entire family in Bolzona and his career eating up a majority of his time, Asher did not have color in his life. He talked all day yet spoke to no one.

With his hair still dripping from the shower, he passed by the stainless steel refrigerator without bothering to eat. It was more than likely that he needed a keeper. Sometimes he simply did not eat or sleep as he should. Most times, it seemed pointless. Dropping across the couch, he stared up at the plain white ceiling. A buzzing noise cut through his depressing thoughts. Asher glanced around attempting to see where the sound came from. Finally, he spotted his phone trying to crawl its way off the table. With a heavy sigh, he went after it before returning to his previous position. Everything cleared away the moment he read the words waiting for him.

So, funny story, I was watching this documentary on coal mining—don't ask. I'm boring. Anyhow, a thought hit me. Does anyone ever call you Ash, or are you always Asher?

Rhys was at home watching TV. He could be anywhere and with anyone, but he chose to stay home. It was ridiculous for Asher to hope it meant anything. Hope never listened to him.

My younger sister is the only person who calls me by that name, so I do not hear it often. Here, I am always the proper Asher. His finger hovered over the send button. At the last moment, he added, *What does one wear for an evening of coal mining programs?*

Once the text went out, Asher stared at the ceiling tapping the phone against his lips. Surely, his question had been a harmless one. Rhys didn't have to answer. He wasn't chasing him...much. The phone vibrated. Asher nearly lost an eye when he sent the mobile flying in surprise and it landed on his face.

"Dumbass," Asher muttered. Rubbing his cheekbone, he silently thanked whoever watched over him that he'd been alone for the incident. He nearly dropped it again when he opened the message. A picture of Rhys from the rib cage up appeared on the screen. A very bare and delicious chest stared out at him. Asher's mouth watered. Lingering on the spot below Rhys' chin a bit longer than necessary, Asher ran his gaze over Rhys' face. A sound emerged from the back of his throat before he could stop it. Those eyes and that smirk, damn, he had it bad. The phone shook again. With a sigh of regret, Asher scrolled past the picture to read the incoming text.

Sorry. It was an impulse. Since you haven't answered, I assume I crossed the line.

How long had he been staring at Rhys' picture? Before he could make things worse,

Asher typed out a quick reply. *I'm the one who should apologize. The sight of your gorgeous form caused my fingers to go numb—in a good way, and I dropped the cellular...on my face.*

Asher wanted to hit himself again. What sort of idiot confessed to such a thing? By the time his phone alerted him to another incoming message, he'd convinced himself Rhys would decide he was too stupid to waste any more time on.

Rhys: *You're in bed then? Damn. I'm missing it.*

Asher: *Not really. I'm on the couch.*

Rhys: *My picture didn't cost you an eye, did it?*

The corners of Asher's mouth lifted. How odd they'd had the same thought. *They are both intact, although one might turn black by tomorrow. How ever will I explain such a thing?*

Rhys*: Let me see.*

Asher snapped a quick shot of his face and sent it off.

Rhys: *As an expert on black eyes, I can assure you it will be fine by morning. I should confess. That was a trick. I only wanted a picture of those sexy eyes.*

Asher*: Should I drop my mobile lower next time?* He really did slap his hand across his forehead after hitting "send" this time. One day soon someone

146

would invent an unsend button, but today wasn't the day. Pity.

With a violent shake, a set of images appeared across the screen of his phone. His eyebrows hit his hairline and he nearly swallowed his tongue. Settling farther into the cushions, Asher scrolled happily through each one. It would be a long, fun night.

* * * * *

A chime cut into the song blaring through the headphones. Rhys pulled his phone out of the treadmill's cup holder. Normally, he would have let the message go until he finished his five-mile run. Before Asher. Spotting the name he'd been hoping to see, he shut down his machine. Everything else could wait.

Asher: *I passed a woman on the street carrying a Mocha Mike's cup. It occurred to me, I could trip her. She wouldn't be much of a challenge. I could simply take it from her. Then I had a better idea. Would you like to meet me there for a cup?*

An image of Asher tripping some hapless woman flashed across his mind. Rhys chuckled. A couple of men who were lifting weights nearby paused to look over at him. He ignored them.

Rhys: *Just tell me when.*

He'd not finished even a quarter of his usual workout, but he didn't care.

Asher: *Twenty minutes?*

Checking the time, Rhys decided he could pull it off if he ignored every posted speed limit.

Rhys: *I'm there.*

He made it in eighteen. At a table near the back of the eclectic coffee shop, Asher stared down at a neatly folded paper. Two women nearby watched him,

148

wearing matching hungry expressions. Rhys felt their pain. He was near to starving for the man as well. The cuffs of Asher's blue dress shirt were rolled up to his elbows, exposing his muscular forearms. Rhys couldn't see the lower half of his body, but he knew from experience it was perfection. Halfway to the table, Asher finally noticed his approach. Rhys almost missed a step. As if a light switch had been thrown, Rhys was back inside Affinity seeing Asher for the first time. Something about the man punched him the gut. He wanted more.

Choosing the chair across from him, Rhys motioned toward his cup. "I hope you paid for that?" A wicked smile pulled at Asher's lips, drawing his gaze. The images—now saved to his phone—taunted Rhys.

Asher dipped his chin. "I did. Would

you like one?"

"Caffeine is not a part of my diet. I'm merely saving you from yourself."

"Ah. I fear I am wasting your time then. The threat has been averted."

Rhys was shaking his head before Asher finished speaking. "Being with you is never a waste."

One of the women at the table next to them waved wildly. He caught the motion out of the corner of his eye. Tearing his gaze away from Asher, he focused on the pair. They were both brown-haired, but the one attempting to gain his attention had green eyes while her friend's were almost the same shade as her hair.

"It is you. Holy shit."

His eyebrows lifted in question. "Have we met?"

"No," she drew out the word as if their having met before was out of the realm of possibilities. "You're Rhys Collier."

"I'm aware." There wasn't a hint of sarcasm in his tone, only confusion.

"You're the US MMA Middleweight Champion."

Understanding dawned. He wasn't used to it yet. "I am," Rhys agreed. A low chuckle sounded from Asher's side of the table.

"Ohmigod!" Her screech was close to ear-piercing. "I was in Boston when you fought Terry Richards for the title. That was an awesome match."

He wasn't sure what to say. "Thank you," he said, deciding to go with the most obvious.

"Can I have your autograph?"

"Depends on where you want it," he answered without thought. Asher choked on his drink.

She raked him with her gaze. Thankfully, whatever she was thinking, she kept to herself. Even though he'd meant he would not be willing to sign anything other than paper, he saw how his words could be misconstrued. "A napkin would be fine."

A napkin and an ink pen slid across the table. Rhys flashed Asher a grateful smile. His eyes were shining with humor.

"I'd love one too," her friend added shyly.

"Sure. Do either of you want it made out to anyone in particular?"

"Beth," green eyes answered immediately. Her friend waited until he'd finished with Beth's before answering. "I'd love it if you could make it out to my son. His name is Connor."

"How old is your son?" Rhys asked while keeping his eyes locked on his task.

"He's ten." Her voice went from bashful to proud as she answered.

Scratching out his name, Rhys handed the napkin over. "You don't look old enough to have a ten-year-old." Her face lit up. He'd not been attempting to charm her. She really didn't look old enough to have a child that age. Nonetheless, he could see she enjoyed hearing it.

"Thank you," she said primly. Folding the napkin, she slid it inside her purse. "We'll let you get back to your..." She paused glancing between him and Asher for a moment before adding, "Coffee. It was nice meeting you." He could tell Beth wanted to say more.

He turned his attention back to Asher before she had the chance. Mouth twitching, Asher quickly lifted his drink to his lips. After a moment, he seemed to pull himself together. "You're very popular today."

Uncomfortable with the topic, Rhys did his best to steer Asher away from it. "As I was saying, this is not a waste. Do you come here every day?"

Asher eyed him carefully making Rhys feel as if he saw too much. "Hmm, very well," he said with a sigh. "I do come here every day. I cannot imagine the torture of a day without caffeine." He paused appearing to think it over. "Actually, I cannot begin to picture what a day in my company would be like without caffeine."

Rhys relaxed in his chair. "For some reason, I get this image of you cursing loudly at an office filled with people while speaking only Italian."

Instead of the laughter Rhys had been hoping for, Asher drew his brows together as if thinking his over his words. "You know, I did that this morning already."

In spite of his amusement, Rhys wasn't one to miss an opportunity. "I can't allow such a thing to happen again. Someone needs to protect the lower level employees in your building."

"Are you offering to meet me again tomorrow?"

Rhys found himself leaning forward, drawn closer as if by an invisible lure. They may as well have been alone for all the notice Asher took of anyone else around them. "Or, I could make you coffee in the morning."

Asher's mouth lifted in one corner even as his eyes took on a wicked glint. "What time are you meeting me here tomorrow?"

"Depends on how late it is when you

send me your final picture tonight," Rhys shot back.

Lifting his cup to his mouth again, Asher's eyes filled with lust. Sensuality dripped from his every pore. Damn, the man possessed the ability to change his expression from hot to cold in a way Rhys had never seen before.

"Perhaps I'd better meet you in the afternoon then."

Satisfaction roared through him. "That's probably for the best," Rhys agreed.

Chapter Five

Asher's home surprised Rhys. Although the location screamed money, the house itself wasn't as obnoxious as Rhys expected. The place wasn't huge. He didn't know much about such things, but the front steps seemed to be some form of marble mixed with stonework. He assumed the combination kept it from becoming too slick when it rained while maintaining the appearance of luxury. He loved it. The woodwork around the door's frame held his attention as he waited for Asher to open it. He'd not bothered knocking. It seemed pointless since Asher had forgotten to mention Rhys would need a code to get through the front gate. It was all good. Not only had Rhys already gotten to enjoy the sexy Italian's voice when he'd called to find out how to enter, he also now had the code saved to his phone. Every piece of information he gathered was an inch of ground he gained toward integrating himself into Asher's life.

The door swung wide. Cool air, soft light, and delicious male cologne enveloped him. Catching a glimpse of a dark t-shirt and blue eyes, Asher occupied his space. Rhys heard the front door close. He assumed Asher had pulled it shut on his way out. All Rhys could do was feel. A muscular chest hit his. Strong hands gripped his hips. Fingers brushed the bare skin above the waistband of his jeans, making Rhys realize Asher had pushed his shirt up an inch. The hard surface of the entryway felt warm underneath Rhys' flattened palms. He didn't care that he was pressing Asher's body against it. The taste of Asher's tongue drove all rational thought from his brain.

Asher moved from Rhys' lips to his neck. His chest expanded as he inhaled. "I apologize," Asher said against his throat. Each word tickled Rhys' skin before heading straight for his groin. "This week has been torturous temptation."

He tried to pull away. Rhys touched Asher's face, stopping him. Holding his jaw, Rhys leaned in one more time, closing his mouth over the bottom lip that had been teasing him for a week. He didn't move to deepen the kiss in any way. It was an attempt to brand the flavor into his memory.

"Never apologize to me again," Rhys growled as he took a step back. "Are you ready?" He didn't want to give Asher time to argue. "We'll probably arrive a bit early for Knox's match. If we don't, we'll never get close enough to see anything."

Asher straightened away from the door. "Let us not be late then."

Awareness of Asher's presence at his side never left Rhys. Not for a second. As he'd predicted, the warehouse where unsanctioned matches were held was packed to capacity five minutes after they arrived. The sound of fists cracking against flesh filled the air. People cheered and groaned with each blow depending upon which side their money rested.

The winner drew more applause than jeers when it ended. The arm raised in victory was covered from wrist to collarbone in an intricate tattoo. Shaggy blond hair dripped with sweat.

"I believe I have seen that gentleman somewhere before." At Asher's statement, Rhys looked closer at the man in question. He turned his head in their direction, almost as if he could feel them discussing him. Rhys dipped his chin in acknowledgment when their eyes met. Kurt returned the gesture.

"You have." Rhys' remark came out sounding dry. "He works the door at Affinity." With a silky chuckle, Asher shrugged. "I suppose it is good I am not as memorable as you."

Turning an incredulous look on Asher, Rhys scoffed. "Are you kidding me? I haven't been able to wipe you from my mind since setting eyes on you."

Asher's eyes shone with mirth. "I meant because of your title." His gaze dropped to Rhys' mouth before returning to his eyes. "In every other way, I am extraordinary."

Don't I know it, Rhys thought, resisting the urge to readjust himself.

"Next up we have Knox Collier. I hope everyone has their bets in." The announcement caused the crowd to push forward. Somehow, Asher ended up at Rhys' back in the crush. His brother's familiar form ducked through the doorway of the cage.

"I would know you were related even if no one said as much. The two of you look very similar." The sound of Asher's voice floated over Rhys' shoulder. The heat of Asher's skin seeped through his shirt.

"Huh. I've never thought about it."

Asher was close enough that Rhys could feel his nod. "The difference is in the countenance. Yours is charming smiles."

"And Knox is hard," Rhys finished Asher's thoughts with a nod. "He had to step into the role of adult at a young age. Rigid living is all he knew before his wife."

"So your parents are gone?"

Rhys nodded. He wasn't ready to have that conversation. Luckily, Asher didn't push for more. He shifted even closer behind him. "My money is on the other guy, by the way." Asher's lips brushed his ear when he spoke.

He didn't touch him in any other way. Rhys' body reacted the same as if Asher had stroked his shaft. In an attempt to call his body under control, he eyed the man in question. His hair had been shaved into some strange design on one side of his head. In spite of his odd appearance, he seemed every bit as fit as Knox. However, Rhys knew the truth. No one was as vicious.

"You're betting against my brother?"

A low-sounding laugh fell from Asher's lips, sending a vibration straight to his already weeping cock. There wasn't a chance in hell of Rhys reeling in his lust. "Not with actual money. Only verbally. The other fellow has a good thirty pounds on him. Not to mention, his reach is longer."

It was true, but Asher had never been to an underground match. He'd also never seen Knox fight. A smile tugged at Rhys' lips as Asher's breath fanned across the side of his neck. "What if we make it a wager then?" Rhys suggested. Turning his head, he brought Asher's face into his line of sight. "If my brother wins, I get to see you again tomorrow night."

Asher's expression never changed but his eyes darkened. "If he loses, you have to come home with me tonight and allow me free reign over your body."

Damned if Rhys didn't hope Knox lost. Lowering his gaze to Asher's mouth, he lingered there for a moment before answering. "You're on."

The bell rang. Rhys turned away. The awareness of Asher lingered. Knox bounced on his toes a moment before clipping his opponent across the side of the head. The crowd pressed closer to the cage in their excitement. Asher's chest came up against Rhys' back. Even with the thunderous cheers and jeers going on around them, he could hear Asher speaking to him quietly. "Are you hard for me?"

The horde shuffled forward as Knox's opponent landed a blow to his shoulder. Asher used the momentum to his advantage, allowing his hips to cradle Rhys' ass long enough for him to feel his desire. Rhys' skin tightened as chill bumps rose on his skin. Electricity surged between them. "Answer my question," he demanded, showing the alpha side Rhys could not resist. "Are you hard for me?"

Tilting his chin, Rhys cut his eyes at Asher as he made his admission. "I'll probably have a permanent limp."

Asher's lips twisted into a sinister grin. "Good. I plan to fuck you. You'll never forget it."

When would this goddamn fight end? As soon as the question ran through Rhys' mind, Knox snagged the back of the dude's neck. With a jerk, he pulled his head down while lifting his knee into the guy's face. The double impact of downward momentum against upward thrust did the trick. With a twist, Knox tossed him to the mat. He didn't move.

"Knockout!" The judge's announcement rang out loudly, sending the throng into cheerful hysteria.

"Peccato. It seems I've lost. I guess you'll have to choose to go with me willingly." Asher paused for half a breath before tacking on, "I have cookies."

A surprised bark of laughter escaped Rhys. "Damn. You don't have to lure me to the dark side. I'm a hair's breath away from exploding inside my jeans just from you breathing on the side of my neck."

"I think I'll have to pass on meeting your brother tonight. As you know, I'm not opposed to a public display. If you're not in the truck in the next five minutes these people will get a much different show than they paid to see."

He made it there in two. There were bruised toes and ribs along the way as he barreled his way to the door. Rhys was beyond caring. His dick was desperately beating against the zipper of his jeans begging to be closer to Asher. Yellow lights flashed as he hit the button on his keyless remote. Asher climbed into the passenger side while Rhys jumped in behind the wheel. He didn't stop there. Rhys kept going until he was pinning Asher against the seat. Something sharp bit into his knee. He hit his elbow on Asher's door. Nothing mattered except the taste of Asher's lips...the sounds of his moans.

The parking lot, while filled with cars, was empty of people since there were matches scheduled for several more hours. Rhys wouldn't have cared even if they weren't alone. His patience was at an end. The back of his head stung where Asher gripped his hair at the roots holding him in place. The rich smell of Asher's cologne teased Rhys' nostrils as he dragged air into his lungs. He was starving. His hunger for Asher was more powerful than anything he'd ever experienced. It was unequaled.

Without waiting for permission, Rhys tore at the button on Asher's jeans. Damn, his mouth made him hot as hell. Rhys wanted more. Traveling south, he nipped at the column of Asher's throat while setting his erection free. His hips left the seat as Rhys encircled it.

"Fu—"

Rhys smiled as the strangled cry died in Asher's throat.

"Tell me what you want," he demanded while snagging Asher's shirt in his teeth and dragging it upward. His sculpted torso came into view. Rhys dipped his head, swiping his tongue over the ridges. Ragged breathing met his question. Rhys froze, refusing to budge until he heard the words. "Say the words, Ash."

"Goddamn you," he growled. "I want you to suck me. I need your hot mouth surrounding— Ugh—" His words died again on a strangled cry as Rhys opened his jaw wide taking him all the way to the back of his throat. "Yes. Damn."

Rhys allowed him to slip almost completely away before repeating the motion. Rhys tightened his throat around Asher's cock.

Asher pumped upward against him. "Fuck me with your mouth. Yes. Suck me off." He held the back of Rhys' hair in a death grip.

The taste of masculine salt and pre-cum filled Rhys' mouth, causing his dick to weep heavily inside his jeans. The sounds Asher made as Rhys' tongue shaped his shaft drove Rhys wild. He wanted to jack off right then. However, he needed Asher's orgasm like he needed oxygen. It was necessary. It mattered. Hollowing out his cheeks, he increased his pace while swallowing him down.

"Take it all. Fuck. I'm going to come."

Rhys sucked hard. A hoarse cry tore

from Asher as a hot jet hit the back of Rhys' throat. He accepted it as his reward, swallowing the thick cream and lapping away any evidence. With a sharp tug, Asher jerked Rhys' head upward and sealed his mouth over Rhys'. He sucked at his tongue before growling against his lips. "Get this fucking vehicle in gear so I can get inside you."

* * * * *

The glass wall across the back of his home that gave him an amazing view of the city had been the deciding factor for Asher when he'd purchased the property. To him, there was not a single thing more beautiful than the Vegas horizon at night. So he'd thought. That was before meeting Rhys. Now, there wasn't any comparison to the sexy man currently occupying his living room.

While Rhys stared out at the city

lights, Asher enjoyed the scenery named Rhys. He was perfection personified. Deep lines of defined muscles caused ripples and valleys across his physical canvas. It drew Asher's hands. He couldn't avoid its lure. The hem of Rhys' t-shirt scrunched in his grip. His knuckles scraped along Rhys' sides as he slipped the material upward. Rhys accepted the loss of clothing without protest.

"Look at you, submissive and sexy as sin. Does this mean I'm allowed to take my pleasure however I choose?" Asher punctuated his question by trailing his fingertips across Rhys' bare torso. His back arched. Goosebumps rose on his skin.

"The sound of your moans makes me think I'm really the one in control here."

The deep hue in Rhys' tone said

more about how turned-on he was than anything else thus far. Asher also understood how he felt. The noises the man made when he came had haunted Asher since their night together. He wanted it again. He wanted everything. He needed Rhys. Underneath him. Above him. Moaning. It was...necessary. Everything felt right and in sync when he was nearby. Asher longed for him. Considering he had not pined for anyone in years, this thing with Rhys wasn't something he wanted to lose.

His chest tightened even as he traced the line of Rhys' abs with the pads of his fingers. Damn. He hadn't been as scared in all his life as he was at the moment. Someone like Rhys could and most likely would crush him. Not that he would allow the knowledge to stop him from stealing every second he could.

Asher's cock lengthened while his hands went to work on the button of Rhys' jeans. When his erection sprang free, saliva flooded Asher's mouth. He could almost taste the pre-cum on Rhys' crown. It would coat his tongue before the end of the night.

The silky skin over hardened steel slid across his palm as he stroked Rhys' shaft. He leaned into Asher's touch. "This is mine. Not just for tonight. Capisce?" Asher couldn't believe he'd said the words. They fell from his lips as if ripped from his chest before he could call them back. He had to know. Better Rhys should destroy him now rather than later. He was already becoming too attached.

A hiss escaped Rhys as Asher added a second hand to his ministrations, cupping his balls. "Yeah. I want more than tonight."

Asher hid his smile by pressing his mouth to the center of Rhys' back between his shoulder blades. He was desperate to feel Rhys' tight ass greedily pulling at his cock. The desire to watch as he came unglued outweighed any other. Even if Rhys walked away, he would never forget him. Asher would ensure it. Rhys would never be able to think of him again without getting hard.

"Let me have the rest of your outfit. I have plans for you."

Rhys complied without question, slipping out of the remainder of his clothing. "Have a seat," Asher demanded, motioning toward the couch. With panther-like grace, Rhys strode across the room and sat down. Asher's dick twitched at the show.

Every muscle in the fighter's body rippled and flexed with every action he made. Rhys was completely comfortable in his skin, as he should be. One day, he would trace every single line with his tongue. It was a promise to himself that Asher intended to keep.

The table in front of the plush, black leather monstrosity Rhys currently occupied was an equally obnoxious expensive dark-gray marble piece. It held Asher's weight as he sat on the edge between Rhys' knees, making Asher thankful for his penchant for overspending. Keeping his gaze trained on the sexy male who stared back at him heatedly, Asher slipped out of his shirt.

"Touch yourself. I want to watch." At his command, Rhys' mouth lifted at one corner. He slid down an inch, widening his knees until they touched Asher's. Strong fingers encircled his cock. Asher watched in fascination as the scarred hand tugged upward. Rhys' head dropped to the back of the couch. His eyes hooded until he was watching Asher through narrow slits. His lips parted on a breath. Asher tried to ignore the pulse beating in his dick. He wanted to squeeze it and relieve some pressure. He wanted Rhys' pleasure even more.

"You're so fucking sexy."

Asher almost broke at Rhys' compliment. The man continuously tested his willpower.

"The way you're looking at me." Rhys sucked in a deep breath. His eyes fell closed for a moment as he stroked himself. When they reopened, they shone almost unnaturally bright. "Damn. You're making it hard for me to hold out for whatever it is you have planned."

Taking a bit of mercy on him, Asher slid to the floor between Rhys' knees. "You always make me hard so it's only fair," Asher admitted. Snagging one of Rhys' wrists, Asher brought two of Rhys' fingers to his mouth. Rhys sucked in a deep breath as Asher curled his tongue around the digits. He loved the way Rhys tasted. Allowing them to slip from his mouth, he slowly guided Rhys' hand until the wet fingers were pressing against his asshole. He didn't leave any room for doubt about his expectations. Rhys didn't pretend to misunderstand. He pushed the two fingers inside. Asher watched, enthralled, by the image of Rhys stroking his large cock while pumping away at his own ass. It was the sexiest thing Asher had ever seen. He wanted more.

"Do you ever do this when you're alone? Better yet, have you fantasized about having me here?" Rhys moaned. "I can do more things than you could ever imagine on your own. For instance, I can do this." Shoving Rhys' hand away, Asher wrenched him forward, spreading him wide, before ruthlessly shoving his tongue inside him.

"Fuck!" Rhys cried out loudly. He gripped the seat of the couch in a white-knuckled hold while Asher teased him without mercy. He knew which nerve endings would bring the most pleasure. More importantly, he knew how to keep Rhys hanging right on the edge of orgasm.

Pulling away before Rhys could come completely unglued, Asher took in the sight of the gorgeous erection begging for his attention.

"How close are you?" Asher asked, dying to know the answer. The look on Rhys' face said he was barely hanging on. The flush on his cheeks enhanced the light in his eyes. His gaze seemed unfocused.

Asher wanted to pat himself on the back, but he equally needed to hear Rhys' answer.

Rolling his balls between his fingers, Asher added, "Is it here yet?" Swiping his tongue up the length of Rhys' shaft, he swirled it around the crown. "Or here?"

"Holy fuck! You're a tease."

The hoarse words made Asher chuckle. "Hmm, you can still talk. I must not be doing a good enough job." Reaching over, Asher slid open a small drawer at the base of the coffee table.

"I anticipated your arrival," he explained as he pulled out a condom and suited up. "I'm hopeful, I suppose," he added, as he popped open the bottle of lube he'd stashed alongside the condoms. He stroked his cock, coating it with the oily substance. He didn't bother wiping it away. Instead, he fisted Rhys' erection, enjoying the sensation of velvet skin over hardened muscle against his palm.

"You're also fucking slow as hell."

Rhys slid closer and set his foot on the edge of the table next to Asher. Unwilling to give him a chance to back down, Asher moved in. Probing the entrance of his ass, Asher sealed his mouth over Rhys'. He'd wanted a lot of things in his life. He felt certain there had not been a single thing he coveted the way he did the man beneath him.

Rhys sucked in a deep breath when Asher pressed his way inside. The tight ring of muscles gave way. Asher stroked his tongue along Rhys'. He murmured things even he didn't understand. All he could do was feel. His body became one large nerve ending set ablaze with electricity. A chant began inside Asher's mind. It was something ridiculous about claiming ownership. There was also a bit of nonsense about being willing to do anything to hang onto this moment. Damn. He was a mess over this man. It was killing him to go slow. Without warning, Rhys gripped his hips, hauling him forward. He impaled himself on Asher's dick.

"So goddamn sexy," Rhys said against his mouth.

Every muscle in Asher's body tensed at the ecstasy rolling down his spine. A hot jet of semen hit his stomach. Fisting Rhys' cock had become a mindless act at some point. A surge of pride and possessiveness roared to life.

Asher needed Rhys to understand what Rhys was doing to him. "You make me want..." He didn't say anything more. There were too many things. Rolling his hips, he wished he could keep jacking

Rhys until he got off one more time. The pressure beat at the head of his dick.

"Come for me, Asher. Fuck. I love the hum you're making in your throat right now."

Proving who was truly in charge of this game, an orgasm tore through Asher on a sharp gasp. Evidence of their encounter pressed between them. Sweat beaded on his skin, rolling down his spine as he slipped free of Rhys' body. The sound of ragged breathing filled his ears. Asher's bottom lip had gone numb minutes earlier from Rhys' biting kisses. However, nothing topped what Asher saw in Rhys' eyes while staring down at him. Cupping his face, Rhys drew him closer. He held onto Asher's gaze as he pulled his mouth to his. Being with Rhys was nothing short of sensual destruction.

* * * * *

An unfamiliar weight across the center of his back caused Rhys' eyes to fly open. The vision of Asher sleeping next to him brought the prior night's events flooding back. He settled back down before accidentally waking Asher. A knee to the spine seemed a small price to pay in exchange for watching Asher unimpeded. He used his arms to pillow his head. A dark lock of hair fell over one of Asher's eyes. He looked peaceful. Rhys' heart squeezed. He wanted to keep him. For the first time in years, he craved something that had nothing to do with the ring or someone who didn't feel the same way he did.

"You're staring at me."

Asher didn't open his eyes. The sound of his voice startled a low chuckle from Rhys. "I don't see how you could know."

A dimple appeared at the corner of Asher's mouth before disappearing again. "I can feel it."

"You're wrong," Rhys blatantly lied. One blue eye peeked open. Asher grunted before his arm snaked out snagging hold of Rhys. At his urging, Rhys rolled, tucking his back against the sexy Italian's chest.

"You smell like chocolate." He could feel Asher's chest shaking with suppressed laughter. "Seriously. I haven't been able to get the smell of your cologne out of my head. It has been driving me nuts. I just realized why. You smell exactly like some sort of spicy chocolate."

Asher shook harder. He pressed his face against the side of Rhys' neck as he spoke. "Go to sleep, Rhys." His demand was heavily laced with laughter. "I promise I won't disappear on you."

At Asher's reassurance, every muscle in Rhys' body relaxed. How was it possible Asher had known exactly what Rhys needed to hear even when he had not known? That thought consumed him until sleep finally stole him away.

* * * * *

A moan fell from his lips at the deep pull on his cock. Wet heat sucked at his dick, setting his body on fire. It was one hell of a way to wake up in the morning. Holding onto the nape of Asher's neck, Rhys fucked his mouth. With his head tilted back, Rhys sawed in and out, touching the back of Asher's throat, before slipping away again. As the pressure built, he stared down the line of his body. Blue eyes met his gaze. The air left his lungs in a whoosh as an orgasm shot through his body. Asher's lids fell closed. The vision Asher presented while swallowing down his seed seared into Rhys' brain. Something shifted in the center of his chest. The need to make Asher happy grew. He knew he would never be able to get enough. Asher's mouth opened over his lower oblique before he swiped his tongue along the path of his abs.

"Damn." Under the man's touch, his erection would not subside. "I need a shower," Asher said against his skin.

"I need to make your head explode." Rhys could feel Asher's smile against his stomach. He climbed off the bed. Even though Rhys was disappointed, he couldn't complain about the view. Asher wore his nudity with the same confidence as he did a ten-thousand-dollar suit.

"Oh," he said turning back to Rhys, giving him an eyeful of his impressive erection. "If you're determined, feel free to meet me in the shower whenever you're ready. There's another bathroom down the hall. There's also an extra toothbrush in there if you'd like."

The second Asher disappeared through the doorway, Rhys shot from the bed and down the hall. He tried to go slow, allowing Asher a bit of space. It wasn't happening. He found himself rushing through his usual morning routine to get back to him. When he crossed the threshold into Asher's private bathroom, steam and the smell of soap hit him in the face.

The walls of the shower were completely clear with only a few designs etched into the glass. They did nothing to hinder his view of Asher with his head tilted back, allowing the water to slip down his body. His hard shaft stood out from his body making the blood pound in Rhys' ears. Almost as if he felt him there, Asher turned his head. Light blue eyes collided with his. Suddenly, Knox's voice floated across Rhys' mind. *"Someday, someone will look at you in such a way you'll be instantly addicted to how it makes you feel."* Damn. He owed his brother an apology.

An expression he could only describe as sinful, crossed Asher's face before he pushed the door open, inviting Rhys inside.

In an instant and without a word, Rhys was there, surrounding Asher with his massive size. He did his best to overwhelm him. With soap-slickened skin and erections slipping against one another, Rhys ended up being the one overcome as their tongues met. Asher swallowed his moans. Rhys knew the exact moment he slipped and fell over the edge. He was powerless to stop it from happening. Nothing had changed. Asher was still out of his league. No doubt, Rhys would end up crushed when the sexy male figured it out. But for now, in this moment, he owned Asher. He would make the most of it.

* * * * *

Rhys caught sight of the Armani tag as Asher pulled the plain black t-shirt over his head. He could feel his mouth twitching. Desperately, he tried to hold back any hint of humor. When Asher released a heavy sigh, he knew he'd failed to hide his reaction.

"Yes. It is ridiculously expensive. I can see you are dying to say as much."

Rhys let loose the smile he'd been holding in. "You do seem to have an addiction to pricey items."

"Where I am from, these items cost four times as much as they do here.

Everything has to be imported in Bolzona, driving up the price," he explained with a shrug. "To me, it is very cheap to live here. However, I do understand I am unico."

Rhys shook his head. "I have no idea what that is unless you're telling me you're a unicorn."

This time, it was Asher holding back a smile. He made a circular motion with his hand as if searching for the right word. "It means I am one of kind. Unique."

"I see I'm going to need an Italian dictionary."

"It does not happen often. Sometimes I forget," Asher admitted with a wry smile. He closed the distance between them, gripping Rhys' hips between his hands. He crowded his space as he confessed. "You make me forget."

Rhys couldn't tear his gaze away from Asher's eyes. No one had ever looked at him the way Asher did. Hungry. Possessive. He wanted it all. His phone buzzed. Asher didn't back away.

"Someone else seeks to steal your attention," Asher said.

"They can wait."

Asher smirked at the growled statement. "I am greedy. You should answer your messages."

"Spend the day with me," Rhys demanded, refusing to budge.

"It might be important. Perhaps you have a family emergency."

"At least have breakfast with me."

His nostrils flared giving Rhys the impression Asher considered doing more than breakfast. "Yes. Now answer your messages."

Giving in, Rhys snatched his phone from the top of Asher's dresser. He scrolled through his options.

Drew: *If you have time today, please stop by No Rival. I'll be here most of the day, and I need to discuss something with you.*

He'd not planned to do anything other than spend time with Asher today. Drew rarely asked for anything. "Do you care if we make a quick detour before we eat?"

"Not at all," Asher answered immediately.

The short drive to No Rival passed in a companionable silence. It seemed neither of them possessed a penchant for unnecessary chatter. Even as Rhys parked in the underground garage and headed toward the club's entrance, Asher followed without a word. When they reached the unmarked metal door, Rhys motioned for Asher to join him at his side. Pointing at the keypad, Rhys punched in the sequence of numbers needed to disengage the lock. "Don't forget that code."

"Too late," Asher admitted sounding sheepish.

Rhys waited for the green light to switch back to red on the panel before going through the steps once more. "I'll text you the passcode, just in case."

"Is there a reason I need to know this?"

At Asher's question, Rhys almost smacked himself in the forehead. He felt so comfortable in Asher's company, it was easy for him to forget the man didn't already know every detail of his life. "This is where I spend most of my day," he explained. "I train here. If you ever need to find me, most likely, this is where I'll be. Seems to me, it's only fair for you to know how to get past security since I know how to get through yours." Rhys added a wink as he pushed open the door.

"Your reasoning escapes me since I can change my code at any time, but I'm not complaining, nor do I intend to bar my door against you."

Rhys could feel the idiotic smile stretching across his face. He was powerless against it. Turning left inside the building, he headed straight for Drew's office. He didn't expect to find him inside since he rarely had the chance to sit down. It came as a bit of a surprise when he spotted the man he was searching for seated behind a mountain of paperwork. Glancing up at their arrival, he waved for them to take a seat in the empty chairs across from him. An obvious sales pitch rang through the speaker of the phone sitting on his desk. Rhys held his silence not wanting to disturb Drew's call.

"It's a lot of money, Drew. I think you should reconsider."

"Yep. Not interested," Drew said, sounding as if he really wasn't. "Look, I have an appointment. I'll have to let you go."

Silence met Drew's words before a heavy sigh came across the line. "All right. Give me a call if you change your mind."

"Yep," Drew said again, cutting off the call without bothering to say goodbye. "Fucking vitamin companies always wanting someone to sell out," Drew grumbled.

Rhys wasn't surprised. "Sometimes it's nice not having a landline. I've avoided most of the vultures because of it." Motioning toward Asher, Rhys added. "Drew Alexander meet Asher D'Ettore. We were on our way to grab something to eat when I got your text," he said, explaining

Asher presence.

Half-rising out of his seat, Drew held his hand out to Asher. "It's nice to meet you."

"You as well," Asher said, sounding genuine as he accepted the handshake.

Reclaiming his chair, Drew turned his attention back to Rhys. "I have a business proposition for you." He trailed off and Asher jumped to excuse himself.

"I'll wait outside."

Rhys reached over, stopping him. At the slightest touch, Asher fell silent even though Rhys didn't say a word or as much as glance in his direction.

"Is this personal business or business, business?"

At Rhys' question, a small grin touched Drew's mouth. The last time Drew had a business proposition for him, Rhys wound up learning way more about the man's personal life than he could have ever dreamed.

"Business, business," Drew answered drily.

"Then Asher is cool to stay here if that's all right with you?"

Drew shrugged. "Whatever you want."

Asher kept quiet and Rhys didn't look over to gauge his reaction. Leaning back in his chair, Drew got straight to the point. "I'd like to hire you to teach MMA classes here." Before Rhys had time to respond to his offer, he added, "Part of the deal would include No Rival as your sponsor for all future matches as long as you are employed here. Of course, this means you would have to move back to town."

At Drew's final words, Rhys went cold. "Did one of my brothers put you up to this?" He knew as soon as the words left his mouth, he'd insulted Drew, by the way his face hardened. As crazy as it seemed, his shoulders relaxed at the knowledge.

"First off," Drew said, beginning to tick off fingers. "This place belongs to me. There isn't a soul alive, besides my wife, who could convince me to put its reputation on the line just to keep you in Vegas. More importantly, you've earned this offer. Middleweight champion is a big deal. Of course, there is some legal stuff involved on the sponsorship end, so you might want to get a lawyer to represent you on that. This is strictly a business decision for me," he reassured him. "I can say No Rival has helped more than one person make it all the way to the top of their weight class. On a personal note, it's getting harder for me to handle the load of sparring match requests. I want to spend time with my wife and daughter. These men want to train against the best. What do I do? If it comes down to a choice, Aubree and Adalyn will be the winners."

Out of the corner of his eye, Rhys saw Asher straighten in his seat at Drew's mention of involving lawyers. Excitement coursed through his veins at the opportunity. What Drew offered was a competitor's dream come true. A huge part of him wanted to jump on the deal before it passed him by. Another part realized Drew was right. Getting legal representation first would be in his best interest.

Tilting his head at an angle, he brought Asher into his line of sight. He was already watching Rhys. A silent conversation passed between them. A smile so wicked, it bordered on criminal, touched Asher's lips. Switching his attention to Drew, Asher transformed from silent companion to ruthless attorney in the blink of an eye.

"I am the solicitor in charge of Rhys' affairs. Have you drawn up a proposal yet on the sponsorship?"

Drew smiled wryly. "That's a question for my attorney. I'm not a paperwork person. As Rhys' friend, I would never screw him over, though. He can trust my word."

"As his attorney, I would recommend against doing such a thing. However, in this case, I was present to hear your offer, and my word carries a great deal of weight inside the courtroom. We will accept your offer, on a temporary basis, in good faith. I see no reason why Rhys couldn't get started on any date that is mutually agreed upon."

"Deal," Drew said immediately.

Rhys wasn't one hundred percent sure what he'd set in motion. Two things were hauntingly clear. All future matches he entered would be for No Rival. Even more importantly, he'd just agreed to stay in town. Lord help him.

Chapter Six

Rhys: *I'm here.*

Asher glanced at the words on the screen of his phone.

Asher: *The door is unlocked.*

With the message sent off, he turned his attention back to the paperwork sitting at his elbow. He did his best to concentrate. The happiness welling inside him made it impossible. Headlights flashed across the security camera, drawing his gaze to the monitor hanging in the corner. With a shake of his head, Asher tried, once again, to focus. He would not watch the sexy man slipping from his truck. Work needed to be done. The numbers in each column didn't add up. They blurred. It took Asher a moment to realize, he wasn't seeing them at all. A shadow fell across the table. Warm lips touched the side of his neck.

"I've been waiting to taste this spot all day long," Rhys murmured against the column of his throat.

"Anything else?" Asher barely restrained himself from telling Rhys how much he'd missed him. Gripping the edge of the table, boxing him in, Rhys dropped his chin to Asher's shoulder.

"That's as far as I got." His admission made Asher feel special. It wasn't a sexual desire Rhys had spent his day craving. It was a longing for contact. He didn't want to hope. Not that it stopped him. "You're still working?"

"If you choose to call it such."

"I didn't have to come tonight."

"You didn't," Asher agreed. Picking through his words, he did his best to hide the longing behind each one. "But I want you here. There will always be more work waiting for completion than I can handle in a twenty-four-hour period. I have only one of you."

Rhys' knuckles whitened. His grip tightening on the wood made Asher want to sigh in frustration. He was not expressing himself as he wanted.

"You're damn right you have only one of me. I don't share." Rhys' growled words caused Asher's mind to go blank.

"You misunderstand. I meant you are more important to me than this. However, now that you've said as much, I feel I must add, I absolutely will not allow anyone else to touch what is mine." He turned his head, bringing Rhys into focus. He held his gaze making sure Rhys understood how serious he was. To his surprise, a smile broke out across Rhys' face.

"Finish whatever you need to. I'm good at keeping myself entertained."

He started to push away. Reaching out, Asher stopped him before he could go anywhere. "It won't be like this every night."

Rhys shrugged at his promise. "So what if it is? What difference does it make if you're concentrating on the TV or paperwork? I'm here. We're together. More importantly," he added, moving in closer. "I get to do this anytime I want." Cupping his cheek, Rhys urged his head back. The gentle brush of lips against his took Asher by surprise. His tongue teased open Asher's mouth. Instead of delving inside, Rhys paused. There was a moment where even the air seemed to hold its breath as they simply shared each other's oxygen. Asher's heart squeezed in his chest. He was falling. Spiraling headlong into emotions he wouldn't be able to control. Their tongues met. It was more sensual than sexual. Everything about Rhys left him wrecked.

Rhys leaned away, swiping his thumb over Asher's bottom lip. The tender look in his eyes stole Asher's voice.

"I'll be here when you're done."

With his promise still hanging in the air between them, Rhys headed for the bedroom. Asher watched him go, still unable to say a word. The way Rhys' cotton t-shirt stretched across his wide shoulders, Asher's palms itched to touch him. Jeans slung low on his hips. Asher's stomach nearly growled in his hunger for the man. It was a sickness. An obsession. He was addicted. When Rhys disappeared from view, Asher tore his gaze away from the doorway. If the stack of paperwork sitting in front of him was what stood between them, then Asher needed it gone. With a resigned sigh, he set to work.

Two hours later, Asher pushed away from the table groaning as something popped in his back. A glimpse at the clock ruined any excitement he'd worked up over spending time with Rhys. No doubt, he had dozed off long ago. Stripping as he went, Asher slipped beneath the covers, doing his best not to disturb the man sprawled across the other side of the mattress.

The light from the muted TV flickered across Rhys' form. Asher spent a moment simply staring at the outline of the body beside him. It was strange to have someone next to him each night. If he lost Rhys, it would kill him.

"I signed up for a match today."

His gaze flew to Rhys' face. He was watching him.

"Did I wake you?"

Rhys ignored his question. "I'm a bit nervous about it."

Hearing Rhys confess to any vulnerability was enough to give Asher pause. "Is there a particular reason why?"

He felt more than saw Rhys shrug. "If I fail, it will reflect on Drew. Before, it didn't matter if I lost. It was all on me, but now, Drew will look bad for having faith in me if I can't win this one. I don't want to hurt a business he's worked hard to build."

Asher weighed his response before offering one. He didn't want to make light of Rhys' fears. In the end, he decided to be honest. "It seemed to me, when Drew made his offer, he was searching for a way to spend extra time with his family more than anything else. Not that he didn't seem thrilled with your talent," he tacked on for good measure.

"I guess." Rhys didn't sound reassured.

"When is this match?"

"In six weeks."

"So you will train hard," Asher said trying a different tactic to soothe his fears. "You will start earlier or stay later until you feel as if you cannot lose."

"That would take time away from you. Think of something else."

His petulant tone almost caused Asher to chuckle, but he managed to hold it in. "Don't worry about me."

The air left Asher's lungs when Rhys pounced. A very pissed-off male stared down at him. "I'm not doing anything that would take time away from you, so think of something else."

"You are nervous," Asher calmly reminded him.

Lowering his head, Rhys nipped at Asher's collarbone. Goose bumps rose on Asher's skin at the sensation. His cock lengthened.

"No," Rhys said against his chest before scraping his teeth over one of Asher's nipples.

"You need to train." His voice had lost some of its resolve, but he wasn't giving in. He wanted to support Rhys. Rhys slid lower. His tongue traced each of Asher's ribs. Continuing his descent, his lips touched Asher's hipbone.

"Ash," he breathed. The way Rhys said his name caused Asher's eyes to fall closed. The power of his emotions was overwhelming. It was more than adoration. His feelings for Rhys went beyond anything he'd experienced before.

"I want to help." The confession came out on a gasp as Rhys closed his lips around the tip of his erection and swirled his tongue around the crown. Rhys pulled away. Cool air hit his wet member.

"You want to help. I want to fuck you. Whatever shall we do? I guess we'd better sleep on it."

Asher growled. He couldn't stop it. The sound rumbled from inside him without his permission. Rhys was a tease.

"How about I kill you instead?" Asher offered in his aggravation. "Then you won't need to be anxious any longer."

A silky chuckle fell from Rhys' lips. "If I'm dead, then I can't do this," he said before swallowing Asher's dick down the back of his throat. Asher's skin felt too tight. Everything from his navel down filled with delicious pressure before landing in his groin. His hips left the mattress, fucking Rhys' willing mouth. Rough hands squeezed his ass. Fingers found every sensitive nerve ending. Hitting the back of Rhys' throat, Asher moaned. The fine threads of his sheets crushed inside his clenched hands. There was no mercy. No more teasing. The pull of Rhys' tongue, the tightening of his throat and the way Asher's dick brushed the roof of his mouth were all setting him ablaze.

Rhys set a pace guaranteed to achieve a quick result. His balls drew up tight. Rhys growled. The vibration sent Asher over the edge. Oxygen rushed from his lungs on a whoosh as an orgasm shot from his cock. Rhys kept him pinned to the bed, taking everything Asher had to give. Tiny laps of his tongue brushed away every drop of evidence. Asher ran his fingers over every spot he could touch. Rhys' hair, his shoulders and each of his knuckles was branded into Asher's brain with each pass. No doubt, he could pick

Rhys out of a crowd of men in the dark. Lips touched his navel. Rhys' bare hip brushed his inner thigh. Asher's skin was one huge nerve, absorbing every brush of skin on skin. Rhys' breath fanned across his chest a split second before his mouth opened over the spot.

"I'll go with you." Rhys froze at the words. Burying his fingers in his hair, Asher tugged, urging Rhys higher. Meeting his stare, Asher added, "If you wish to train later," he clarified. "I will go with you and we shall spend our time together there. If you can entertain yourself while I work, I can do the same for you. As you said, we're together. It doesn't matter where."

"You'd get bored."

"Watching you sweat?" Asher asked, unable to keep the disbelief from his voice. Running his hands up the hard planes of

Rhys' back, he swallowed down a moan. Rhys was every bit as delicious to the touch as he was a treat for the eyes. "I think boredom will be the least of my worries. You demanded I think of something that would not take away from us. This is my solution."

"You're amazing."

The adoration in Rhys' voice caused Asher's heart to skip a beat. "I'm incapable of staying away." Asher almost bit his own tongue in an attempt to stop the words from falling from his lips but he couldn't.

"Good." Rhys' quick response soothed away some of Asher's fear. He didn't stop there. "I wouldn't let you, even if you tried. I'm infatuated." He touched his lips to Asher's. "Completely hooked," he added, tracing the lines of Asher's mouth with the tip of his tongue. "A bit desperate to own you," Rhys confessed, delving inside. The moment of shock Asher experienced at Rhys' admission died a fiery death. It was carried away on the wave of overwhelming desire Rhys sent flooding through his veins.

Chapter Seven

Five weeks later

I have a sparring match scheduled for tonight. Meet me at No Rival?

Rhys sent off the text hoping Asher didn't mind spending another night hanging out with him at work. It made sense for him to do a majority of his training during the nighttime hours. Most of the men he could spar with worked full-time day jobs, making it hard to schedule any practice time during those hours. Even knowing that, if Asher couldn't make it, Rhys wouldn't stay. He would not take time away from him due to a case of nerves. Asher's immediate reply set him at ease.

Yes. I will be there in ten.

It amazed Rhys how his entire mood

swung upward at the knowledge he would see Asher soon. Ten minutes seemed closer to twenty while Rhys worked on his abs. Of course, he'd been eyeing the clock the entire time. It seemed just as watched water wouldn't boil, the hands of a clock didn't move under his stare.

There were two sparring areas inside No Rival. One resembled a regular boxing ring while the other was set to standard cage match specifications. Due to the high demand for practice time, each one had to be reserved in advance. Rhys managed to snag the boxing area for the next two hours. It helped that he was now the one in charge of keeping track of the waiting list. Finding an opponent was the easy part. It seemed everyone wanted to work with him now that he held the title. Not that Rhys was complaining. He needed to train against the best if he hoped to stay on top. The boxing ring was his preferred zone due to the low-impact padding. He needed to stay in shape, but the last thing he wanted was an injury. The risk increased substantially inside the cage.

Rhys suspected Brian Johnson would one day be his toughest competition. Going with his hunch, he'd accepted Brian's practice challenge. Equally matched in height and weight, if Brian made it to the top, he'd be in the same class as Rhys. Best he should learn the man's moves now rather than in a real bout. A motion near the front entrance caught his attention. Rhys spotted the six-foot-three, mocha-skinned Brian first. A bright smile stretched across his lips leaving Rhys frozen with shock. He couldn't remember ever seeing the man—whose deadly stare and pierced eyebrows caused people to cross the street to avoid him—smile. Brian glanced in his direction, nodding, before returning his attention the person responsible for his good humor. Following the line of his gaze, Rhys caught a glimpse of Asher. He spoke animatedly holding Brian's attention in a way Rhys had never seen before. Damn, no one was immune. Rolling to his feet, Rhys gave up on his crunches while eating up the sight of his sexy male in action.

A maroon dress shirt with the sleeves rolled up to the elbows showed off Asher's relaxed side. The dark gray dress pants proved he'd not been home yet for the evening. Turning his head, Asher noticed him watching. With a wink, he returned to listening to whatever Brian was saying. A spike of pride ran through Rhys. Everywhere Asher went, gazes followed. His accent made heads turn.

Anyone he spoke to wanted more of his intelligence. He belonged to Rhys.

With a quick shake of hands, Asher headed in Rhys' direction. Brian held up one finger before pointing toward the locker rooms. Nodding his understanding, Rhys gave Asher his full attention.

Leaning over the ropes, a hint of teasing slipped into his tone. "I can't let you out of my sight for a second. All these guys are just waiting to pounce the moment my back is turned."

Exactly as Rhys hoped, Asher's eyes shone with humor. "Ah, you are a jealous one."

"I am," he agreed immediately. "But in this case, I'll let it slide since I happen to know Brian is as straight as they come." Asher's eyebrows shot up. He could see him holding back a laugh. Rhys knew right then Asher was hiding something

221

from him. "Okay. Spill."

Snagging hold of the lower rope, Asher pulled while rocking back on his heels. The playfulness didn't leave his face. Rhys almost hated that he needed to work. He wanted to go home with Asher right then. It lasted for half a minute before another thought sneaked its way into his mind. "Wait. Are you attempting to distract me? Oh my God. You've dated Brian, haven't you?" Rhys didn't really believe it. He made sure Asher knew it by asking the question in his best is-this-a-conspiracy stage whisper.

"Nope. It's attorney/client privilege." Asher glanced over Rhys' shoulder then back to his face warning Rhys of Brian's return.

"I'm finding this shit out," he promised. Taking a bit of mercy on him, Rhys held up his phone. "Will you hang onto this for me?"

"Of course," Asher agreed, catching it easily when Rhys tossed it down. He slipped it in his front pocket. Nodding toward a nearby metal folding chair, he added, "I'll hang out over there."

"All right." He waited until Asher was striding away from him before calling him back. "Ash." Rhys could see he was still attempting to hold in his laughter as he reversed his steps until he was standing at the edge of the ring again. Leaning over the rope, Rhys lowered his voice for only Asher's ears. "As soon as I'm done here, we're going home."

"I assumed as much."

"Yeah, but here's the thing—I need you considering all the possibilities, not just the going home part."

Asher released an exasperated sigh. The sound caused Rhys to chuckle.

"Go do your thing or we will never get out of here."

Instead of doing as Asher instructed, Rhys continued holding his stare. He wanted to bury his nose against Asher's throat. Inhaling his scent while absorbing the heat of his skin is what drove Rhys each day.

"You ready to do this or what?"

With one last sweeping glance of Asher's body, Rhys tore his gaze away. He faced his opponent. "Yeah. I'm good to go."

Rhys ran through a quick list of the rules while Brian nodded his understanding of each one. "The biggest thing to remember is this—I am trying to help you. For me, this is not about beating you or you besting me. If either of us ever gets to the point where we have nothing left to learn, then we need to quit."

With his mouth guard in place,

Rhys was unable to give any further verbal instructions. However, he did stop several times to correct a few of Brian's holds. The man worked hard at his technique. Unfortunately, fifteen minutes in, Rhys has already taken him down six different times in ways that would have ended an official bout. Holding onto his patience, Rhys spit out his mouthpiece.

"You're better than this, Brian."

With a growl, Brian scrubbed his hands over his head. "Sorry. It's been a hell of a day. Give me a second." He tilted his chin up, staring at the ceiling as if attempting to clear his head. Rhys used the time to steal a glance at Asher. To his surprise, he found him deep in conversation with Drew's wife, Aubree. She sat at Asher's side chatting happily while Adalyn stood braced on her knees facing the ring. Something that appeared to have at one time been a cookie smeared her face and hands. She couldn't have looked happier.

Brian audibly blew out his breath capturing Rhys' attention once more. He appeared a little more than disheartened. "Shit, Rhys. I hate that I'm wasting your time like this."

He didn't know what to say. It was obvious something was going on with him. Rhys wasn't as good as Drew at helping the men personally as well as professionally. The two things did go hand in hand. If a fighter's head wasn't on straight, it affected their performance in the cage.

"It's just another day," Rhys rushed to reassure him. "I have seven of them per week."

Crossing his arms over his chest, Brian cut his eyes in Asher's direction. "I know you're busy. Hell, even your lawyer has to rearrange his schedule to meet you here."

Rhys didn't bother correcting him. At the moment, it was more important to break down Brian's walls than to stake a claim.

"By the way, you picked one hell of an attorney to represent you. He's one of the best out there. As a matter of fact, he handled my mom's case when she got sick after working on a project for this huge corporation. She couldn't breathe right any longer afterward. Came to find out there was asbestos all throughout the building she was helping to strip clean. The company knew about it ahead of time. They chose not to disclose the information to their subcontractors to save on cost." A small smile touched Brian's lips. "He didn't charge her a dime for his services."

Rhys had never been more proud of Asher than he was in that moment. "I'm sure he doesn't realize how much it meant to her, especially now, since she's back in the hospital. Those bills pile up quick. A settlement doesn't mean much once those vultures get hold of you. It was the principle of the thing, though."

Several speeches about family coming first ran through Rhys' mind. He dismissed them all. Instead, he settled on something simple. "If your mom's in the hospital, you should be there. This shit can wait."

Brian lifted his shoulders in a helpless gesture. "They didn't decide to admit her until about an hour ago. I hated to cancel on you on such short notice. Plus, at this point, there's really not anything I can do."

Waving off his words, Rhys made a

dismissive sound. "Don't worry about it, ever, seriously. It's not a big deal to move things around. Go see your mom."

With a nod, Brian flashed him a grateful smile. "Are you sure you're okay to reschedule?"

"Yeah, man. Get out of here." At his order, Brian finally seemed to take him at his word. With a quick pat on Rhys' shoulder, he dipped under the rope and slipped away. Rhys didn't bother to watch him go. Asher filled his mind. He didn't talk much about his work. It was a fact Rhys took as part of the deal. There were hundreds of privacy things to which he had to adhere. He shouldn't have been surprised Asher would help someone simply because he was in the position to do so. It was almost funny. Every time Rhys thought he couldn't fall any deeper in love with the man, he did.

The thought got his feet moving. The tiny blonde-haired woman who Drew managed to convince to marry him was beautiful enough to stop traffic. Rhys barely spared her a glance when he reached their side. "Why do the two of you look like you're up to no good?"

At his question, Aubree shot to her feet while settling Adalyn on her hip. "We were discussing the charity event No Rival is hosting this Sunday. I extended an invitation to Mr. D'Ettore." Her explanation came out in a rush, and she quickly added. "I'm so glad you've finished early. Drew is tied up in his office, and I need to get going. Would you mind watching Adalyn until he's finished his call? I wouldn't ask, but I'm already running late."

Rhys didn't hesitate. "Sure. It's no problem." Before he could reach for

Adalyn, Asher came to his feet, placing himself between them.

"This little girl is covered from head to toe in some sort of mush. Let me have her. Rhys can grab something wet to clean her up and not ruin his clothes."

"Good idea," Aubree agreed, handing her daughter over without flinching. "I got busy talking about this weekend and forgot about that dang cookie."

Asher held Adalyn to his chest as if there wasn't a single speck of dirt on her. "It seems to have made her very happy so I wouldn't worry about it."

The pair fussed over Adalyn oblivious to Rhys' complete shock. Asher's outfit, minus the tie and jacket, still cost more than most people's cars. Yet he worried over Rhys' sweat-covered clothes. The shirt and shorts he wore were at least four years old. He was also fairly certain he'd not paid more than twenty dollars apiece for each one. With a shake of his head, Rhys left them alone while he went in search of something to clean up Adalyn with. Every movement he made felt forced. It was hard for him to concentrate on anything except the one thought chanting inside his head. Asher was amazing.

Snagging a handful of paper towels, he ran them under the faucet, getting them as wet as possible. On his second pass by Drew's office, Rhys' thoughts had cleared enough for him to notice Drew's open door. Peeking in, he caught a glimpse of the bald fighter sitting with his chin resting in his palm as he listened to the voice droning on through the speakerphone. He couldn't have looked more bored. Sizing up the situation, Rhys made a quick decision. Rapping his knuckles on the wood of the door, he snagged Drew's attention. At the man's nod, Rhys said the three words sure to get the man's ass moving. "Aubree needs you."

* * * * *

Somehow, not only had Rhys managed to get Adalyn cleaned up in record time, he'd also returned with Drew on his heels. Although Asher had been content to spend a few hours at No Rival, if need be, he couldn't deny he was glad for the chance to steal Rhys away for himself. Rhys held his silence until they made it to the parking garage. He'd seemed preoccupied for most of the night. Asher chalked it up to his worries over the upcoming competition. He was doing his best to support Rhys, but he was at a bit of a loss.

"Why don't I leave my truck for the weekend? If you're coming with me on

Sunday, there's no sense in taking separate cars."

The sinister smile tugging at Asher's lips popped up without his permission. He didn't bother hiding it. "You will be at my complete mercy all weekend. I can find no fault with this plan."

A low chuckle slipped from Rhys even as he slid in the passenger side. Wicked thoughts crowded Asher's brain. It seemed he wasn't alone in his plans. The moment he settled behind the wheel, Rhys swiped his hand up his thigh. He left it there. Asher's first instinct was to act. However, the need to have Rhys alone won out. Keeping his gaze locked on the road, he maneuvered out of the garage while attempting to ignore how Rhys' touch affected his body.

"Your teasing will get us killed," he said when he realized his hopes of

234

blocking out the sensation were fruitless.

"I'm not teasing." Rhys' words sounded matter-of-fact causing Asher to shoot a quick look in his direction. There was an odd expression on Rhys' face. There wasn't time for Asher to decipher it at the moment. The second Asher turned his attention back to his task, Rhys added, "It's hard for me to be near you without touching you in some way."

"You are quite necessary to me, as well," Asher agreed. It wasn't exactly what Asher wanted to say. It would have to be enough for now. Rhys possessed too much of everything already. Asher's heart—most likely—would simply be one more in his collection.

"For the record," Rhys said, tearing Asher away from the bleak thought, "the only reason I'm not teasing is because I wouldn't risk your life in such a way. As soon as this car is in park, well, that's a different matter altogether."

Asher fought the urge to break the speed limit at Rhys' threat. By the time Asher pulled into his garage, he was ready to roar his frustration. All the money spent on technology and there still wasn't a faster way for people to get home. Rhys grabbed the door handle, but Asher was too quick for him. Reaching over, he snagged Rhys' t-shirt. The cotton balled in his fist as he towed Rhys over to his side of the car. A flash of surprise crossed Rhys' features before Asher opened his mouth over his. The feel of Rhys' bottom lip against his tongue assuaged some of his impatience.

There were times when Asher caught himself manhandling Rhys, and he was completely incapable of controlling his reaction. It was almost as if he wanted to physically bend him to his will. In the moments when Rhys surrendered, Asher knew the man returned his feelings. Every other second of the day, Asher feared he did not.

Rhys' mouth moved from Asher's lips to his jaw before traveling to his throat. Keeping his eyes closed, Asher focused on the sensation of the air leaving Rhys' lungs as it skirted over his skin. Rhys sucked in a deep breath, releasing it slowly, as if he knew exactly where Asher's head was.

"I need a shower." The brush of Rhys' lips against his neck as he spoke caused Asher's impatience to roar back to life.

"Not as badly as you'll need one by the time I am finished with you."

"I didn't say I was going alone."

Not until the cool marble touched

Asher's back did the buzzing inside his brain ease enough for him to focus on the moment. Steam filled the air. The contrast of hot and cold seemed extreme to Asher's over-sensitized system. Although Rhys stood only an inch or so taller than he did, his wide frame made it seem as if the man was everywhere when he used his body to invade Asher's space.

With his palms braced against the shower wall on either side of Asher, Rhys pumped against him, causing a delicious friction between their touching cocks. Their mouths clashed. Asher held onto Rhys' hips, tugging him closer, even as he enjoyed the feel of Rhys' bones rotating beneath the skin. It wasn't enough. Their tongues fought for supremacy. Asher did not want it to stop. Pulling away slightly, Rhys cupped his jaw with one hand while slipping the other between their bodies. In one broad sweep, he brushed his palm over both of their erections.

Asher loved the expression Rhys wore. Eyes unfocused, lips swollen, he owned those things. Rhys' voice sounded harsher than usual in his lust as he confessed, "I don't want you to get off like this."

He knew from experience he would not. It didn't matter. This had still become one of his favorite things to share with Rhys. It was almost impossible for him to take a shower alone anymore. If he did, his hands would automatically travel south. Asher had once sworn to Rhys he would ruin him for all others. It turned out he was the one who was now useless. He would never again touch himself or anyone else without Rhys lingering there in his mind.

"Where do you want me to get off?"

His question was one of desperation. Need clawed at his skin. His arousal bordered on pain in its intensity. Every single one of his senses was attuned to Rhys. The taste of him lingered in Asher's mouth as his eyes feasted on his body. The sounds of his indrawn breaths and the smell of his skin drove Asher insane. There wasn't a nerve in Asher's body that wasn't aware of Rhys. Reaching over, Rhys switched the water off. Without a word, he stepped out of the shower, pulling Asher along in his wake. The cool air chilled the water on his skin. Asher barely registered the sensation. The muscles flexing in Rhys' back as he moved with a panther-like grace held Asher captivated. The moment they reached the bed, Rhys stopped. He didn't allow Asher the same choice. Pulling Asher past him, Rhys pushed him down onto the mattress.

Rhys' face went hard. A muscle ticked in his jaw. It was beyond fucking sexy. Switching his gaze to the ceiling, Asher flattened his palms against the flat surface at his back. They itched with the need to reach for him. Rhys prowled the perimeter of the bed, almost as if he couldn't decide where to start. It was sweet torment.

When Rhys reached where his head rested on the opposite side of the bed, Asher was unable to stand it a second longer. He fisted his shaft. It was an open taunt. Rhys didn't back down from the challenge.

"That is mine," Rhys growled.

Straddling the mattress on either side of Asher's head, Rhys brushed his crown across Asher's bottom lip. Asher willingly opened for him even as he continued stroking himself. When Rhys hit the back of his throat, he leaned forward pushing Asher's hand away. Before Rhys could take him into his mouth, Asher made his move. With a twist, he rolled Rhys onto his side. The new position allowed him the freedom he needed to open his throat and swallow him. Even as Rhys released a low moan, he tugged Asher's hips forward. With a quick swipe of his tongue, he licked a wet line down Asher's length. His muscles clenched. Even as he reveled in the feeling of Rhys sucking him off, he gave back as good as he got. Pleasure beat at the head of his dick. Pressure crawled up his balls. None of it compared to the emotions squeezing his heart. There were moments when Asher knew he'd follow Rhys anywhere. He was simply incapable of being without him. While he wasn't paying attention, he'd fallen in love.

Chapter Eight

The charity event at No Rival was, for the most part, a closed affair. It was also a world away from the boring crap Asher had to attend in his line of work. No doubt, the money raised at every tedious dinner he'd attended helped the organization it was meant for, but he'd never gone to anything such as this. This was personal. Drew Alexander was well known for his work with critically ill children. When Make a Wish contacted him about a child who wanted to be an MMA champion for a day, the men had jumped at the opportunity to make his dream come true. Only a handful of reporters were allowed to attend, along with family and close friends of the members involved. Asher—unsure of what to expect—had claimed a seat in the corner upon arrival. He'd not moved since. The action on the mat kept him engrossed.

The chance to watch Rhys completely unguarded was a rare treat. He was the type of person who everyone, and no one, knew. People saw exactly as much as Rhys wanted them to and nothing more. He smiled and tried to please everyone, but he kept none of life's joy for himself. Asher wanted to fill him with all the happiness he'd been denied. The knowledge gained strength with every passing moment he spent in his company.

The man who owned ninety-eight percent of Asher's thoughts stood in the center of the caged-in ring, pretending to go down hard as the little boy—who couldn't weigh more than thirty pounds—tackled him around the knees.

Asher laughed harder than anyone did as Rhys flailed underneath the boy who pinned him to the mat as if the child's strength was too great for him.

The media ate it up. Asher could see Rhys was truly enjoying himself, and the little boy was happy. That was all that mattered. With the middleweight champion beaten, it was Drew's turn to take on the tiny fighter. As Rhys stepped—with an exaggerated limp—from the ring, a blonde reporter moved into his path before he could make it ten steps.

"Rhys, would you care to comment on the recent rumors surrounding your private life?"

Asher wanted to growl, but Rhys didn't appear the least taken aback by the woman's question. A slow grin spread across his face and Asher bit back a smile. He knew that wicked expression. Nobody stood a chance against the sexy fighter's massive charm.

"This is a children's event," he

gently reminded her. A blush touching her cheeks was the only sign his remark hit home. Unfortunately, she didn't run away. Dropping her voice an octave until there could be no doubt of her intentions, she moved an inch closer to Rhys.

"Maybe afterward then..."

Rhys' eyes hooded. A hint of heat entered his expression as he stared down at her. It was sexy as hell, but it was also fake. Asher knew every one of Rhys' scorching glances as well as he knew his own reflection. He swallowed down his laughter as the woman's eyes glazed over. Asher felt her pain. Rhys was too much of everything.

"As tempting as your offer is, I'm taken, so I'll have to pass."

She sighed before attempting to cover the sound with a cough. Rhys turned his back on her, catching Asher's gaze. A tiny smile hovered on his lips. Oh yeah, Rhys was taken. He'd better never forget it.

"Ten minutes," Rhys mouthed. Asher's heart raced. He was a few short minutes away from having him by his side. Rhys headed for the locker room. The reporter followed him with her eyes but didn't attempt to stop him again. As soon as Rhys was out of earshot, the woman turned her attention to the man following her around with a video camera.

"I hope it's not true. It would ruin his reputation."

The balding guy appeared to listen with only half-an-ear. Nonetheless, he still nodded in agreement at her words. "Yeah. Nobody wants to cheer for a gay champion."

Asher's hands clenched. He couldn't have heard them correctly. Shit. He'd not considered what people would think of Rhys. The pair disappeared but their conversation lingered inside him. It wouldn't happen. There was no way in hell Asher would allow any damage to Rhys' reputation. When he was in court he was playacting. He could pretend in public. He was good at that. No one ever needed to know about them. Fuck. He couldn't give him up. For all his strength, Asher was not that strong.

Rhys reappeared dressed in his usual street clothes. Claiming the empty seat at Asher's side, he flashed a grin. A dimple appeared in his cheek and Asher moved closer despite his earlier convictions. When Rhys was nearby Asher forgot everything else. Slumping in his seat, Rhys threw his arm across the back of Asher's chair. To all the world, he might appear relaxed, but Asher could feel the power rolling off him in waves. He cut his eyes at him. Rhys' smile widened.

"Hey sexy, what's your name?"

A snort escaped Asher at Rhys' question. He was outrageous. It was addictive. "Yours," Asher answered before he could stop himself. Rhys' eyes darkened and his voice deepened showing a hint of his lust.

"Damn straight. Now, what's a guy got to do to get you alone?"

"So, do you have this under control for the next couple of hours?"

Drew's sudden appearance caught Asher off-guard. It was a bit of ice water in his face after the reporter's comments.

"I do. No worries." Rhys answered Drew's question without a hint of discomfort over Asher's presence at his side.

Asher leaned away keeping his face

devoid of all emotion as he carefully turned his attention to the phone balanced on his knee. He no longer knew how to act.

"Mr. D'Ettore, I think I should look into hiring you to manage my stuff. The attorney I have now, I can't even get on the phone without scheduling an appointment two weeks in advance, but I see you everywhere."

Asher politely tucked the mobile inside his jacket. Focusing on Drew, he offered the man a bland smile. "I'd be more than happy to discuss it with you. Mr. Collier has all my contact information. If you give my secretary a call, she'll set you up with an appointment."

Drew chuckled at his response. His gray eyes shone with mirth. "Damn. You're putting me off on someone else already? I guess I'll stick with the lawyer I know then."

Rhys' gaze moved between them. His brows drew together showing his confusion, but he didn't question the sudden change in Asher's demeanor or the use of the title. Holding onto his business-like manner, Asher nodded.

"If you should change your mind, I'm sure Mr. Collier will let you know how to get in touch with me." Damn, there was the title again. He couldn't seem to stop. "Now, if the two of you will excuse me, I have another appointment scheduled today." He needed air.

Drew apologized the moment Asher stood. "I didn't mean to interrupt." Asher waved off his concerns. "Think nothing of it. Our business is complete. Please feel free to avail yourself of my empty seat."

Drew shook his head. "Thanks for the offer, but my wife is waiting for me. I only wanted to stop by and make sure Rhys didn't need me to stay for a little while longer."

Out of the corner of his eye, Asher could see Rhys attempting to catch his gaze, but he kept his face averted. "In that case, it was a pleasure seeing you again." Unable to stand it a moment longer, he focused on Rhys. Dipping his chin in a quick nod, he made his excuses. "I'll have to leave you now, Mr. Collier. Until next time...," he trailed off.

Rhys' face went hard. "Yep."

On that bleak note, Asher made his escape, refusing to look back. He would not be the reason Rhys lost everything he'd worked so hard to achieve. No matter how much it hurt.

* * * * *

Drew's eyes followed Asher as he left. Shaking his head, he turned his attention to Rhys the moment Asher was out of sight.

"You know, when I wear a suit, I imagine I feel the same way a dog does while wearing a sweater. It's unnatural. But that dude, he reeks of old money and class. I feel a bit like I should stand up straighter or something."

"Yeah," Rhys said for lack of anything else. He was beginning to see Drew didn't need any real encouragement to keep talking. His wife had once told Rhys that Drew was a motor mouth. He'd not believed it at the time, but the last few months had proven how wrong he'd been.

"I can't even imagine having the kind of cash that had people questioning their posture."

Even in Rhys' shocked state, he found Drew's statement ridiculous. "All you have to do is show up to an event and it's worth a minimum of two-point-two million. So, exactly how much money can you not imagine having?"

Drew's smile reminded Rhys of a mischievous child. "Old money," he answered before adding, "How much do you think he's worth exactly?"

Rhys thought Asher was priceless. Unfortunately, it didn't appear his opinion counted for shit. He shrugged. "I don't know. I'd guess maybe four of you." When would this conversation end? No one ever noticed when his world was falling apart. Drew released a low whistle. Rhys couldn't hold his words back. "I never realized you were such a gossip."

"A regular old hen," Drew agreed. "Anyhow, Aubree really is waiting for me, so I'd better get going."

Without Drew's presence to distract him, Rhys' mood darkened by the second.

He managed to hold it together until he made it to his truck two hours later. The moment he slid behind the wheel, his hands shook in some form of delayed ultra-shock. His breathing felt labored as if he was sucking each lungful through a straw. They'd been seen together in public hundreds of times. How had he never noticed? Every moment they spent together ran through his mind. Had Asher ever touched him openly? He honestly couldn't recall. It seemed as if he had, but when they were together, the rest of the world disappeared, so he couldn't remember if anyone else had been nearby. There was only Asher. He could have sworn there had never been any signs of secrecy. When he looked at Asher, even the power of his gaze caressed Rhys' skin. Maybe that's why he'd never noticed anything lacking.

However, after the incident with Drew, he couldn't lie to himself. Asher didn't want anyone to know about them. His phone vibrated in his pocket, and Rhys maneuvered it out.

Asher: *I really did have a business meeting.*

It took Rhys three tries to read and understand the text message through the red haze of rage coating his vision. *Yep. Got it*, he texted back.

Asher: *Truly. You know how my schedule can be.*

How was it possible for Asher to be so intelligent yet so ridiculously stupid at the same time?

Got it. Even as he hit reply, he wanted to throw his phone out the window. The man wanted to pretend they weren't together in public then he shouldn't know him in private. Rhys didn't hide. Ever.

Asher: *Good. I did not want you to worry. Come see me tonight.*

Rhys ignored the message. The balls on this dude. Exhaustion landed heavy on his shoulders. He'd agreed to stay in this town and work for No Rival. He would keep his word but damned if he didn't regret it now. Every fucking time he thought things were looking up, he got pushed back down again. Maybe he needed to simply learn his place and quit dreaming. His chest hurt. Some people never found happiness.

"Guess I'm one of them," Rhys said the words aloud, hoping it would help him accept them. Nope. It was still sitting there on his windpipe cutting off oxygen to his brain. Ten minutes passed where Rhys couldn't force himself to move. He needed to go home, but the will to do anything seeped out him. Since meeting Asher, he'd spent every night with him. For that reason, he'd not bothered searching for a place of his own. Where was home? It hadn't been an intentional move. He'd simply not wanted to be anywhere else. Now, he was left with the option of a hotel or going back to Mandy and Knox's. In his current mindset, he wasn't sure that was such a good idea. He was a little afraid of himself.

Asher: *I'm sorry.*

The two words appearing across the screen confirmed Rhys' every fear. He knew. It wasn't only Rhys looking for problems where there were none. Asher fucking knew what he'd done.

Rhys: *You know what? No worries. It's all on me. I shouldn't have let you get inside my head.*

He turned his phone off the second the message went out. There was nothing left to say.

Chapter Nine

The French roast was bitter today. Almost as if it sought to mimic Asher's mood. Nothing tasted the same any longer. Everything he put in his mouth curdled once it hit his stomach. Losing Rhys defied description. His image in the mirror each morning matched the one he'd seen prior to meeting the man who'd broken him. It surprised him every time. The pain inside him, while crippling in its weight, appeared to be invisible to the naked eye.

"Peccato," Asher murmured as he touched his cup to his lips.

"Do you pity the coffee this morning or do you always talk to yourself?"

He almost choked. Thankfully, out of necessity for his career, Asher was good at keeping his expression blank.

"It was an observation of life in general. I merely forgot people could see me as it was happening." Asher snapped his teeth together on the last word. After a horrified moment of reflection, he was forced to concede, he had indeed just said that aloud. He tried to fix it. "I mean—"

Kurt chuckled, cutting off his explanation. "I'm sure you meant you are not used to people understanding Italian. Therefore, you feel free to say whatever you are thinking without notice."

Asher thought it over. "No," he decided after a moment. "I stand by my earlier statement. Your theory makes me out to be an ass. I'd much rather people think I am insane."

Kurt waved his cup toward the empty seat across from Asher. "Do you mind if I join you? If you're not sitting alone people will simply think you are speaking with me rather than to yourself."

It was odd. When Asher had seen Kurt fighting in an unsanctioned bout, he'd looked very different. Hardened perhaps. In the coffee shop where Asher spent his mornings with Rhys, Kurt appeared subdued, almost sad.

"Please, do join me. Although I must point out, if you're sitting here, I am technically talking to you even if I'm not."

Slipping into the chair, Kurt trained his green eyes upon him. They seemed even lighter up close.

"Did that statement make sense in your head?"

Asher ran it through his mind once more before answering. "It did. Although, I am willing to admit it did not sound as logical when it left my mouth."

He was a gentle giant. Asher wasn't sure what caused his sudden but sure knowledge of Kurt's character. The massive amount of tattoos combined with his large frame was off-putting. However, if Asher knew anything, it was how to read a person's face. Kurt was a kind soul.

"It's strange."

Kurt's brow drew together proving his confusion over Asher's broad statement. "Are you back to talking to yourself again?"

"Still musing over life," he explained. "It is funny how you never notice someone— until you do—then you see them everywhere. Possibly, we've been in the same place hundreds of times, yet I never saw you before Affinity. Now, I see you everywhere."

Kurt's expression shifted. His lids lowered, hiding his thoughts. He'd not been quick enough. Asher caught the way the man's gaze had moved to his mouth.

"Where is your man this morning?"

Asher's lips parted in his surprise. No words came. Kurt didn't wait for them. "Unlike you, I know exactly how many times we've been in this same coffee shop." Asher's shock was so thorough, he didn't know how Kurt continued to ignore it. Somehow he did. "So, I ask again, where is your man this morning?"

He was helpless to stop the admission. "He is no longer returning my calls."

Kurt relaxed in his chair. Slinging his arm across the metal rungs of the empty seat next to him, he no longer bothered hiding his lust. He lifted his cup to his lips, keeping his eyes trained on Asher. "Peccato."

"So you do speak Italian," Asher said in an attempt to change the subject.

"I speak several languages. There

are many things I do well."

Asher didn't miss the insinuation. He'd promised Rhys there wouldn't be anyone else. Rhys was gone. The truth caused him to drop his gaze to the table. He couldn't hold Kurt's intense stare.

"I assume you'll be at his match tonight."

Thankful for something else to think about, Asher shook his head. "I don't see the point."

"You should go." Kurt's response surprised Asher enough for him to lift his chin once more. Kurt had leaned forward while he wasn't watching. He was close enough for Asher to see the way his green irises streaked with amber. The full-sleeve tattoos, pierced nipples clearly showing through the t-shirt straining across his wide chest, and gauges in his ears kept Kurt from being handsome in the traditional sense. None of those things could mask the sexuality oozing from his pores. "Once you see him, you'll know for sure if it's over. People such as Rhys, they move on without a backward glance. When you see him tonight, you'll recognize the truth. The same thing happened to me once. Someone gave me hope then ripped it away. I could make you forget." He let the words hang between them for a moment, before continuing. "Go see his fight then come find me at Affinity. I promise you won't remember his name by morning."

"And if I decide things aren't over after seeing Rhys?" Asher had to ask.

"Then I will meet you here again tomorrow morning. We will pine for someone else together." Kurt stood without waiting for Asher to comment. Sliding a card across the table, he kept his fingers on top of it for a second. Asher glanced down, taking note of the silver ring on his thumb. There was also an Egyptian symbol tattooed across the top of his hand. He tapped the card. "Here's my number. In case Affinity is not really your thing, you'll know how to get in touch with me. I'm not asking for anything."

"If you're not asking for anything then what are you after?"

Leaning down, Kurt spoke close to his ear. "There isn't a doubt in my mind. You know exactly how sexy you are. I want to fuck you." A hint of cinnamon wafted over Asher. "My motives are purely selfish, but I'm very, very good. You wouldn't regret it. Do I need to pretend I am after something more? I'm not above it."

Turning his head, Asher brought the man hovering over him into focus. He wanted to be immune to Kurt's allure. "I appreciate your honesty." The space he invaded belonged to Rhys.

Kurt flashed a quick grin. It was easily the wickedest thing Asher had ever seen. "Don't lose my number. You'll need it." With his promise ringing in Asher's ears, Kurt walked away leaving Asher staring after him wondering what the fuck had just happened.

* * * * *

It was almost strange the people who showed up at Grid Iron. They would simply stand at the counter and flip through the magazines as if Kerry ran a salon instead of managing a fitness center. Kurt was a rare visitor, but not so much so that Kerry questioned his presence. It didn't hurt that she enjoyed staring at his body. She'd tolerate a lot of things for a hot man. They were her kryptonite.

Twenty minutes passed where the

only sound in the room was Kurt slowly flipping through the pages of his magazine. Finally, he broke the silence. "I spoke to a certain sexy Italian we both know this morning."

Kerry only knew one of those. There was something about his tone. No. No. No. Her brain did not want to accept it. Unable to keep the horror from her voice, she growled. "What did you do?"

Kurt shrugged. "Nothing." Before she could breathe a sigh of relief, he immediately ruined it by adding, "Yet."

"No," she said in an exaggerated whimper. If anyone in the world was Rhys' equal in the sexual destruction of others, it was Kurt. While Rhys would charm the clothes from people's bodies, Kurt used confusion to his advantage. Most people never saw it coming. He left them off-kilter. His bad boy appearance coupled with a gentle nature stunned others long enough for him to slip beneath their radar. Once he was in, he hit them with everything he had. Considering his arsenal included edgy looks, a muscular body, and a way with words that was unrivaled, they were powerless against it. She'd never tasted the wares, but she'd heard stories of his skill. Chill bumps rose on her skin. Asher was in so much trouble.

"He belongs to Rhys." She wasn't sure it would matter. If there were lines Kurt wouldn't cross, she'd never seen them.

"Not anymore."

"Kurt," Kerry cried, adding a high-pitched wail to her voice. "You cannot steal my brother-in-law's lover." She shook her head as she realized what she said. "Scratch that. I know you can, but I'll be really sad if you do."

If he was at all moved by her words, he didn't show it. "For once, I had nothing to do with it. Rhys has stopped answering the man's calls."

"Shut the fuck up."

Kurt shrugged at her horrified denial. "His loss is my gain. I don't intend any harm. With that said, I also will not pass on a good thing due to any misplaced sense of family loyalty on your part."

It took Kerry a moment to decide how she felt. From the beginning, she'd told herself she wouldn't get involved past the initial introduction. Now that the moment arrived, she was failing the test. She'd practically gift wrapped the perfect man for Rhys. Better yet, she'd delivered him already unwrapped. Fuck this. She knew exactly how to feel. She was pissed off.

"I'll kill him."

Kurt scoffed. "I hardly think bloodshed is necessary."

Once again, there was something about Kurt's tone. It seemed a bit too helpful. Kerry narrowed her eyes at him. Why had he chosen to warn her of his intentions instead of simply taking what he wanted? Unless, he meant for her to intervene. His expression gave nothing away. Damn it. Even knowing his game, she was powerless against it. He was like some sort of rock star at addling people's brains.

"You're a romantic at heart, aren't you?" she asked, taking a stab in the dark.

His expression still didn't change. "Don't cast aspirations on my character. I'm simply clearing the playing field of all opponents before setting up my next move."

It was an art form, Kerry decided, even as she gave in. "Fair enough."

She watched it happen and couldn't figure out how he managed to leave her confused about his intentions. In the grand scheme of things, this issue had little effect on Kerry's life. She could only imagine how Kurt impacted someone's heart. He could easily make a person insane.

"What's it like inside your head?"

She'd not meant to ask the question. In fact, she sort of wanted to punch herself in the face the second it left her mouth. There was a genius in his maddening ways. She really wanted to know the answer. A smile—devastating in its wickedness—spread across his face.

"It's dark, but there're chains, paddles and a ton of other fun things, so it's all good."

Holy shit. She just bet it was.

* * * * *

From his vantage point, Rhys had a good view of the ring. He hadn't expected to be able to see a thing considering the huge mob in attendance. Fortunately, they all pressed as close as possible to the steel wire, leaving the space near the back where his private waiting room was located, almost empty. Rhys did his best to hide his surprise when he spotted his family in the crowd. If there had ever been a time they'd all showed up to support him at one time, he couldn't remember it. Dane, Kerry, Mandy, and Knox all gathered near the edge of the cage. As short as Kerry was, she ended up being the first one to see him. She tugged at Dane's arm to get his attention. He glanced in Rhys' direction as she spoke near his ear. Breaking free of the group,

274

she weaved her way through the throng. She'd never make it. Snagging the attention of a nearby security worker, Rhys sent him to fetch Kerry before she ended up crushed.

He'd intentionally avoided her since the disastrous Grid Iron incident. Sometimes things weren't anyone's fault. Other times everyone was guilty. He wasn't sure yet which category they fell under. Her smile seemed strained when she finally reached his side.

"Thanks for sending help."

"What sort of brother would I be if I let you fend for yourself?" It was an asshole move. He knew it. She winced at the question.

"Can we talk?"

"We are," he pointed out. He didn't know why he couldn't give her an inch. There was something about Kerry that always made him want to strike first. Perhaps she saw him too clearly. She eyed a group of women who were inching closer.

"Don't you have some private room or something? You know, to get dressed or whatever?"

Blowing out a breath, he motioned her forward. The moment they were alone, she went straight for the gut.

"Why aren't you answering Asher's calls? He really cared about you, damn it. I swear. You're such an ass—"

Rhys' temper hit the roof. "Goddamn it, Kerry," he half-yelled, cutting her off. "Did it ever it occur to you that maybe I'm the one who ended up crushed?" Throwing his arms wide, he added. "What do you want from me? Obviously, you needed to see me bleed. Well, here it is. You've seen it. Are you

276

satisfied?"

To his surprise, her eyes filled with tears. With a growl, he tilted his head back. A moment of staring at the ceiling calmed him.

He finally asked the question that had been eating at him. "What did you hope to gain?"

"Your happiness." Her voice broke on the confession. She cleared her throat. "I swear, I never meant—" She broke off as if she couldn't go on.

A sad smile tugged at his lips. "No tears when I get my heart broken," he reminded her. "I promised."

Kerry blinked rapidly and the tears gathering in her eyes slid down her cheeks. She didn't bother swiping at them. "You sacrificed your happiness for Knox and Mandy. There was this small part of me that almost expected you to jump in at the wedding and try to stop it, even though they were already married, but you didn't. You stood there at your brother's side. It killed you. I could see it, but you did it." Casting a desperate look around the sparse room, she headed for the only chair. It was an uncomfortable steel folding chair, but she sank down onto it as if it were her last hope in the world. She stared at her hands while she spoke. "Your expression, it reminded me of exactly how I felt the moment they started shoveling dirt into my first husband's grave. It's a silent pain so loud, you think you'll go deaf."

Her words shocked Rhys to his core. They didn't know much about each other, he realized.

"What happened to him?"

"He was killed in a motorcycle accident. I became someone I didn't know any longer after his death. There were several times I didn't think I'd ever feel anything again."

"The thing with Mandy and Knox, I can't fault anyone for that," he heard himself admitting in the face of her sharing. "The better man won."

"You're a good man too, Rhys. You deserve happiness. When I made that bet with you, I really had no idea what I would do. Obviously, there was no way I could act on it, but I also couldn't stand there and do nothing. As soon as Affinity popped in my mind, for some reason, I thought of Asher. I don't know if you know this, but it was his first time there, as well."

Rhys dropped his gaze to the floor. He had not known. Not that it mattered, except it did.

"He's been a member at Grid Iron for as long as I have worked there. We've been friends for the same length of time. When I called him, he was horrified." Kerry chuckled as if she was picturing the moment in her head. "But, I said, don't tell me you don't have some kink in you. All those business suits and the stuffy proper language are hiding something. I'm willing to bet money when the door closes on your bedroom, you swing from the light fixtures."

In spite of everything, Rhys snorted. He would have given anything to have been a fly on the wall for their conversation. "I can't believe you convinced him to do such a thing."

A mischievous smile touched her lips. "He said, 'I will have you know, I would never have something as gaudy in my home as a light fixture sturdy enough to hold a full-grown man.'"

She did such a good impression of

Asher, Rhys could picture him saying it.

"I told Asher, 'You have to see this guy. He has the most beautiful brown eyes and the most gorgeous soul I've ever seen. If you get there and you don't want him, give me the signal. I will figure something else out, but if you don't go, you'll miss out on the greatest guy ever.'"

Rhys swallowed hard past the lump growing in his throat. He'd thought she hated him. She'd given him the greatest gift in the world.

He had to clear his throat twice before finding his voice. "It really was addictive, you know?"

She scrunched up her forehead showing her confusion. "What was?"

"Having Ash love me in return," he explained. "My whole life, I've never had that. I didn't have parents who loved me, and my brothers fell apart under the strain. It has always been only me. Then came Ash." He froze incapable of speaking another word.

Kerry shook her head. She came to her feet. "I don't understand, Rhys. You love him and he loves you."

"He's ashamed of his feelings for me." Rhys let the words fall between them before he lost the courage to force his tongue to shape the syllables needed to say them. Now that they were hanging in the air, Rhys felt a sharp blow in his gut. It was one thing to know the truth quietly inside his head. It was another to say them aloud and give them life.

"Why would he be ashamed?"

A man wearing a bright-yellow special event shirt stuck his head in the door. "You have five minutes, Mr. Collier."

Rhys nodded and waved the man away.

"We ran into Drew. Asher pretended he was meeting me for business. Then he brushed me off as if I was only a client as he ran out of the building."

"Asher? Really? That doesn't make any sense. He doesn't have any reason to hide anything. He's open about his life and sexuality. Why would he do such a thing?"

Rhys headed for the door. He couldn't be late for his match. "It's me," he told her. He paused right before stepping through the doorway. "Nobody in their right mind would openly love someone like me. But for the record, he completely owned me. Heart and soul, they were his. He didn't feel the same and if I've learned anything in the past year, it's that I can't make people do anything. I am damned tired of trying."

Leaving Kerry behind, he snagged one of the members of the security team charged with escorting him to the ring. With the instructions given to help Kerry back to her seat, he forced his mind to go blank. On the march to the cage, he counted backward from a hundred. Looking neither right nor left, he focused on his opponent.

They'd met before. It would end the same. Announcements blared through the speakers. The noise of the crowd became a buzz in the back of his head. They were alone as far as Rhys was concerned. Rules were read. He didn't hear a word of it. Didn't matter. He knew them by heart. Rounds set at five minutes. No pussy moves. He had it.

His opponent went by the name of Williams. It was his last name, but if Rhys had ever heard his first name, he couldn't recall it. An unkempt beard covered the bottom half of his face. It helped keep the man's emotions hidden.

Since Rhys was pissed off at life in general for being such a suck-ass little bitch, he didn't feel the need to hide his emotions from a damn soul. The bell rang. Williams bounced on his toes. Rhys didn't feel up to dancing. Instead, he rushed the mat, closing the distance between them, landing a solid right hook to the dude's cheek. The crowd audibly cringed at the sound of Rhys' fist connecting with bone. Once his initial burst of anger passed, he remembered why he never used that move. If he didn't knock his opponent out in one blow, it would really piss them off. Which is what happened with Williams. He came at Rhys with everything he had.

Rhys prided himself on his ability to judge the outcome of a match within the first few seconds. This match would end in tap out or knock out. Points wouldn't mean a damn thing. They were both too angry. Their emotions were making them vicious in their attacks. Rhys swiped at Williams' legs, but it didn't have the result he'd been hoping for. Instead, Williams had been ready for the move. Using Rhys' momentum against him, he tackled him to the floor. Before Rhys could gain purchase, Williams had him pinned on his stomach and was sitting on his spine while yanking his head backward. The move twisted his body into a painful position.

The temptation to tap out rode heavy on Rhys. The pressure on his spine increased. Straining upward, he made another attempt to unbalance Williams. Time seemed to slow. The shifting of the restless crowd held him transfixed. A young guy decked out in Goth stepped to his right. Just like that, Rhys was staring at Asher. Unlike everyone else surrounding him, Asher didn't move. Their gazes collided. There wasn't a single hint of emotion on Asher's face. It didn't matter. His presence gave Rhys strength. With a short jab above his head, he caught Williams across the ear. When the move caused him to attempt a block, Rhys rolled, unbalancing him. He didn't stop until he reversed their roles. With Rhys now on top, he used every ounce of strength pulling Williams' chin high while sitting on his spine. The palm tapping the mat sent a roar through the building that caused Rhys' ears to ring.

Shooting to his feet, Rhys searched the crowd with his eyes. When his gaze landed upon him, Asher dipped his chin in a quick nod. The official said something Rhys didn't hear, but he dutifully raised his arm when urged to do so. Asher had shown up then he turned his back on Rhys. Weaving his way through the mad crush, Asher headed for the door. Rhys wanted to call his name and beg him to stay. The blow of watching Asher leave nearly caused Rhys' knees to buckle. He'd not let Drew down. The title still belonged to him. Once more, Rhys had managed to prove to himself he was worthy of his place in life. None of it meant a goddamn thing.

Chapter Ten

It wasn't over. The fantastic view from his living room no longer brought him peace. Everywhere Asher looked, he saw Rhys. His ghost drove away Asher until each night, his hours at the office became later. Seeing Rhys, holding his gaze, those things had been his undoing for the past two days. Asher absently ran his fingers along the slight ridges of Kurt's card while staring at the corner. There was an invisible line in the sand. If Asher chose to step over, there would be no going back. Things would truly be over with Rhys the moment he called Kurt. He slid his phone closer. Could he take the final step? Rhys didn't want him any longer. His fingers curled around the receiver. All it would take was the push of a few buttons. He could burn his bridges while still standing on them. His self-destruction would be complete. The door to his office flew open. With a regretful sigh, he dropped the handset back in place. One day he'd remember to lock up on time.

D'Ettore & Bronson was not a large enough establishment to contain the fury Asher saw in Kerry's expression as she stormed inside. His chair creaked as leaned back. Gripping the armrests, he watched her pace the length of his desk. Somewhere in the back of his mind, he'd been expecting this. Even though they'd been friends for years, her new family tie to Rhys left her loyalties divided. Not to mention, she had every right to her anger. He welcomed it. Any punishment she deemed fitting would not be enough as far as he was concerned. He'd denied Rhys publicly. Even the thought of it made him sick to his stomach. It didn't matter he'd wanted to save Rhys from scorn. The look on Rhys' face wouldn't leave Asher's mind.

With each pass, Kerry allowed her fingers to slide along the surface of his desk. Asher focused on the motion to keep from confessing everything. *"I shouldn't have let you get inside my head."* Those words haunted him. He'd let Rhys into more than his head. It took him a moment to realize Kerry had stopped pacing. Instead of the explosion he'd been expecting, Kerry's tone was questioning.

"Has it occurred to you to wonder as to why no one has managed to snag Rhys permanently? He certainly isn't lacking in any way."

Thrown off balance by her inquiry, he said the first thing that popped into his head. "I assumed he had not met his match." It was an honest answer.

However, he barely stopped himself from adding, *before now.*

A sad look passed over Kerry's features. "Oh, he's met his match."

Asher tried to hide how the information crushed his soul. His brain screamed that he was Rhys' other half, but his tongue refused to give up his secrets. Thankfully, Kerry took mercy on him by continuing without encouragement. "You see, Rhys fell in love once. He did what he knows how to do, keep quiet. He expected her to reject him since everyone always has. I don't know how much you know about his childhood. It wasn't good."

"I only know his parents have passed."

"Hmm," Kerry said noncommittally. "That's not exactly true. His mother is alive and well, somewhere or another. She left when he was a baby and his father killed himself a year or so ago."

Asher attempted to make a few sympathetic noises while his heart broke for Rhys. Kerry waved them away. "He's much better for the loss, trust me. The problem is, he didn't expect the woman he fell in love with to care about him. After all, no one has ever openly wanted him."

Asher scoffed, but the somber look on Kerry's face caused the sound to die in his throat. "You can't be serious?"

"Well, have you seen him? God was in a very good mood the day he created Rhys. I imagine fear would freeze your lips together even as he set your body on fire. How could anyone feel good enough to hang onto him?"

He couldn't argue with her logic. Wasn't it why he'd stayed quiet? "Yes. He is the type who makes you want to hear him declare himself. Otherwise, you're only another in a long line of fools."

"Exactly!" Kerry cried. "Can you imagine what it must be like to be trapped inside his head? To him, it must seem as if he's never, ever quite good enough for anything other than warming someone's bed. Do you know this is why I chose you?"

"Your reasoning escapes me at present."

Kerry flashed a mischievous smile. "I knew he would love you. How could he not? You're an amazing person. More importantly, I truly believed you were strong enough to claim him. The person who screams their love for Rhys, without an ounce of ignominy, will end up with the sexiest, most faithful man in the world. It's a shame I was wrong about you."

A surge of anger ran through him. "What in the hell is that supposed to mean?"

Kerry's face hardened showing her true feelings. "When your test came, you were like everyone else, embarrassed by having lost your heart to him. I can't imagine the blow he endured when he realized it. His pain is so much deeper than most because he gives away every ounce of happiness and keeps none for himself."

It was true. He'd seen the shadows inside Rhys, but he'd be damned if he continued allowing her to believe he was in any way ashamed of loving Rhys. "I wanted to protect him from disparagement. He lives a very public life, in a world of harsh men," he said, attempting to make her understand.

Kerry's dark scowl said more than words could. It didn't stop her from trying. "Have you ever seen Rhys give a fuck what anyone thought? He doesn't care about those men. What matters to him the most is you. Not to mention, he's too damn nice. Being mean to Rhys is like kicking a puppy. I might argue with him nonstop, but I wouldn't bother if I didn't care. Knowing how much he's done for Dane over the years, he has my loyalty forever. He's my brother by marriage now, so I'm allowed to give him shits, but most people would rather bite off their tongue than say a cross word against him. He doesn't need you to protect him or buy him things. He doesn't need you for anything, except he needs you."

"I don't know how to fix things," he admitted. "He won't talk to me."

"You know exactly what needs to be done. If he won't talk to you, then make him listen. The time has come to show off some of the alpha he fell for. Go take back what belongs to you. Quit allowing him to run roughshod over you." Her features softened. "It just so happens, I know exactly where he is."

Asher worked at keeping his face clear of all emotion. When had he decided to lie down, allowing Rhys to walk away without his say so?

"I'm listening," he said when she didn't tell him straightaway. Her smile screamed of triumph at his words. "No Rival."

Asher glanced at the clock. Aggravation crawled over his skin at the late time.

"Still? At this time of night?"

"Yep." Kerry's satisfaction over his obvious anger could be heard in the way she emphasized the final "p" in the word as if taunting him.

He ground his back teeth together to stave off his growing anger. He shouldn't ask. It would only piss him off further. "Has he been there all day?"

"Yep."

Asher ran his tongue over his front teeth behind pursed lips, feeling his eyes narrow. The fuck Rhys would kill himself while Asher had any say over the matter.

Pushing his chair away from the desk, he stood. "He needs a keeper."

At his growling tone, Kerry's smile hitched up a notch as she agreed. "Indeed."

* * * * *

One. Two. Kick. Three. Four. Knee. Five. Six. Back kick.

Drew appeared over his shoulder. "How much of what they're saying is true?"

Rhys kept his eyes locked on the bag. "Does it have any influence on my position here?"

"Of course not."

Drew's immediate answer eased some of the tension in Rhys' shoulders. "Honestly? I haven't exactly heard what they are saying, but I can guess, and yeah, I imagine it's all true."

Rhys landed two more blows and a round kick to the bag before Drew reacted to his answer. "Huh. At least I don't have to worry about you ending up as my son-in-law or some shit."

Knee. Left hook. Right hook. Kick. Rhys felt the need to point out the obvious. "Adalyn isn't even two years old yet."

"My guess is you'll still be every bit as overwhelming in seventeen years as you are now."

Drew's answer surprised him enough that Rhys finally snagged hold of the bag, holding it in place as he focused his full attention on Drew. "You've lost me."

The gigantic fighter looked distinctly uncomfortable with the conversation. He shifted from one foot to the other. "Well, you've always been a bit of a player, but if you prefer men then you wouldn't be interested in my daughter."

A bark of laughter fell from Rhys' lips without his permission. "So that's what they're saying? Dude, you can't put a label on me. I want what I want. If I see someone I feel like going after, then I do." He shrugged. "Hot is hot. It doesn't matter to me if it's a man or a woman." To him, the words made perfect sense. He'd never been able to understand why people limited their choices to only one sex.

Drew being who he was, didn't judge or question Rhys' logic. Instead, he chose to turn back to the topic at hand. "Something has the media riled."

"I have the title now," Rhys pointed

out. "Nobody cared what I was doing before." He was dodging, of course. He knew exactly what stirred things up, or rather who.

His private life had always remained behind closed doors because he'd never cared enough to display anyone publicly for long. Until Asher. He mattered. Damn, he couldn't breathe. Why wouldn't the sexy lawyer get out of his head? All the "if only" questions bounced off his brain. If only Asher hadn't tried hiding their relationship. If only he felt the same as Rhys did. The scent of his cologne, the texture of his expensive suits while clenched in Rhys' hands and the sounds Asher made in the back of his throat. All of those things were slowly driving Rhys insane, but he straight up refused ever to be anyone's dirty secret. That thought sent another sharp pain shooting through

301

his chest. It didn't help matters that Drew was eyeballing him as if he could read Rhys' mind.

"You must have been seen with someone if you've got them talking. I mean, otherwise, they wouldn't have any reason, right?"

The memory of the final time he'd taken a shower with Asher suddenly flared to life in Rhys' head. He'd run his thumb along Asher's bottom lip while he'd panted out a breath. That delicious mouth haunted Rhys' dreams. In an attempt to cling to his sanity, he tried harder to concentrate on Drew.

"Wow. Every day you find a new way to shock me with your busybody tactics."

Drew's shoulders lifted proving how unconcerned he was over Rhys' opinion. "I'm just trying to figure you out."

"Nothing to work out here," Rhys

said, wishing Drew would go away and leave him to his slow death. "What you see is what you get."

"What I see is a friend twisted up in knots over someone. None of the other shit matters."

Rhys looked away. Damn Drew and his observant nature. "Yeah. There's someone," he admitted. He couldn't bring himself to say Asher's name. "It's over."

He could see Drew rocking back on his heels out of the corner of his eye. "Doesn't sound to me as if it's over."

"Yeah, well," Rhys said noncommittally as he watched Brian, along with a few of the guys, lingering nearby trying to pretend as if they weren't hanging on every word.

"You know, for a guy who fights for a living you're not much of a fighter. I don't think I've ever seen you have to work to get or keep anyone."

The panicked look in Asher's eyes, when he'd said his final goodbyes flashed through Rhys' mind. *He's embarrassed by me.* He absolutely would not say the words aloud again. "I think I'm just—"

The words died on his lips when Asher's form filled the mouth of the hallway. Rhys blinked a few times to make sure his eyes weren't playing tricks on him. Even then, he considered he might be hallucinating except Brian's eyes fixed upon the man as well.

The shock of seeing the very man who was the topic of their conversation inside No Rival kept Rhys' feet glued to the floor. His tongue stuck to the roof of his mouth. Asher's determined stride and fierce expression held him completely captivated. Everything else around Rhys ceased to exist. Asher's steps never faltered. Rhys couldn't look away. Decked out in his usual business attire, the unbelievably expensive suit could not have looked more out of place than it did in that moment, but damn. He was gorgeous. Anger, lust, and frustration showed clearly in Asher's gaze. He didn't look away from Rhys' face as he bore down upon him.

What is he doing here? No sooner had the question pinged off his brain, than Asher snagged Rhys by the neck, hauling him forward. He slammed his mouth over Rhys' with enough force that their teeth bumped. It didn't matter who was watching when Asher curled his tongue around Rhys'. Every ounce of longing, hurt, and emptiness Rhys had experienced since losing Asher showed itself in their bruising kiss. The fine thread of Asher's jacket balled in Rhys' hands when he tugged the man who remained the center of his obsession flush against his body. It wasn't anywhere near to being close enough. He wanted to be under his skin. It was only fair since Asher was under his.

Asher growled against his lips. "Never, ever have I been ashamed of you. To me, you are amazing." Rhys' throat tightened at Asher's admission. "You do not answer my text or return my calls. You will talk to me now, or as I've warned in the past, I am not above a public display. I grow tired of being ignored."

A sardonic smile pulled at the corners of Rhys' mouth at Asher's threat. His accent had grown thicker, showing how angry he truly was. "I think it's too late." If people were getting a show, he didn't care. Asher's expression had him hypnotized.

Misunderstanding Rhys' words, Asher's eyes flared. "Fine. I will speak here then. You are mine, and I am proud to say as much. You may go out of town to compete making all the TV reporters sigh with your charming ways, but you will come home to me. Furthermore, you will not let me hear of you working yourself into the ground as you have done this day. Capisce?"

Rhys worked hard not to laugh. He did not think Asher would appreciate it. A ridiculous burst of happiness ran through him at Asher's demands making it hard to stamp it down. "Got it," he agreed.

At his acquiescence, Asher sealed his mouth over his once more. With one last nip of Rhys' bottom lip, he pushed away. "You are busy. I will allow you a few minutes longer to finish up. Then you will come home. Ciao," he called over his shoulder as he strolled away.

Shaking off the spell of Asher's skill, Rhys finally glanced around. Brian kept his eyes averted but a tiny smile hovered on his lips. Drew still lingered at his side. With his massive arms crossed over his chest, he eyed Rhys carefully, waiting until Asher disappeared before speaking.

"It doesn't seem things are over after all."

"Guess not," Rhys agreed, trying his best not to smile like an idiot.

"Damn boy. You snagged a sugar daddy."

"Yep."

Drew's eyebrows rose. "And you're still here, why?"

"That's a damn good question," Rhys admitted as he peeled off his grappling gloves.

* * * * *

For all his bravado, blood pounded in Asher's ears. He'd not been sure at all. If Rhys' had turned him away, damn, he couldn't even think about it.

"Ash."

The sound of his name brought him up short. His hand paused on the handle of his car door. Turning his head, he spotted Rhys bearing down on him. Before he had time to react, he was against the car. The taste of aroused male filled his mouth as Rhys fell upon him. He was everywhere. His lips moved from his mouth to his throat. Rhys murmured against his skin.

"Go straight home," Rhys said.

"Not going to make it," Asher admitted without an ounce of shame. Between the adrenaline running through his system and the built up frustration from having been too long denied, Asher nearly went up in flames at the mere hint of satisfaction. There were very few cars in the underground garage besides Rhys' and his, but anyone could show up at any moment. It wasn't a good time. After a quick glance around, Rhys eyed him carefully, as if assessing how serious his confession had been. His eyes darkened, making Asher want to know what he'd seen on his face.

"Open your jacket."

At Rhys' command, Asher's already hardened cock wept in anticipation. He didn't question the order. The jacket fell open. Bypassing his belt and button, Rhys went straight for the zipper of his pants. "Do your best to block us." Without further warning, he set Asher's erection free and fisted it. Leaning in close, Rhys used his large frame to hide his actions while Asher did the same. Pressing in even tighter, Rhys touched his lips to spot beneath his ear. "If we were anywhere else, this would be in my mouth." He punctuated his promise by tugging upward and squeezing near the tip.

Asher's knees nearly buckled. His balls were heavy. His spine itched. Every nerve in his body needed Rhys. Saliva filled his mouth at the thought of tasting him.

"I would curl my tongue around you, tugging at your soft skin with my taste buds before swiping over your crown." He mimicked his words with his hand, swiping his thumb over Asher's crown, and wetting it with his pre-cum. "All this saltiness belongs to me." Dropping his forehead to Asher's shoulder, he brought his thumb to his mouth. He licked away the moisture. "Damn, you're delicious. Have you been thinking of me while touching yourself?"

Asher had lost the ability to speak. He could only feel. When he didn't answer, Rhys stroked his shaft, bringing him closer to orgasm, while continuing to torture him with his words. "I have. I've been reliving every moment we spent together. Inventing new encounters that haven't happened yet. The sound you make when you hit the back of my throat, I want to hear it now." Increasing his pace, Rhys did his best to force Asher to give him what he sought.

Asher fought for breath as he strove toward release. "Sei bello."

"Not as beautiful as you. Not as beautiful as you'll be when you're straddling my waist with my dick buried to the hilt inside of you. Come for me, Ash. Nothing is more beautiful than the sight of you right now. Goddamn, I have missed you."

Black spots appeared in his vision as his balls drew up tight. Semen shot from the head of his cock. Snagging the tail of his shirt, Asher did his best to keep from ruining both their clothes. Only Rhys' strength and the solid surface at his back held him upright. The ecstasy rolling down his back and twitching in his dick stole every ounce of his strength. Even as he gasped for air, Rhys watched him with such hunger, he was ready to go again.

"I love you," Asher confessed. His words came out in a rush. "I do not wish to share you or sleep another night without you. You are unique to me. Prezioso."

Rhys seemed almost held in suspension as he stared into Asher's eyes. He realized something monumental. Kerry had been telling him the truth. No one had ever openly loved Rhys before. Asher did. It was more than love. It was more powerful than anything he'd ever experienced before. He'd meant what he said. Rhys was unique. Unequaled.

His expression gave nothing away. Asher thought he might have heart failure before Rhys finally spoke. "As you said, I have to travel some for competitions. I can't avoid it, but I'd like for you to come with me when I do from now on."

Asher's heart soared at the words. "I would be proud to cheer you on from your sidelines or whatever it is called."

Rhys visibly fought back a smile at his answer. "My corner," he supplied.

"Yes. That thing."

"I don't want to spend another night away from you, ever again, for any reason. I don't care where we sleep. Wherever it is, it should be our bed." Rhys was saying everything Asher dreamed of hearing.

"Good because this is what I demand of you. I should have made my intentions clear much sooner. My only excuse is, loving you has made me very stupid. I want to make you happy, but I cannot read your mind, so I try to second-guess you. I will not do that any longer." He knew he was rambling. He couldn't seem to stop. Twice he'd used the L-word and Rhys had not. Vulnerable and exposed were feelings he was not enjoying.

"Yes, you will. You will try to guess which things make me the happiest, even as I attempt to do the same with you. There will be times when we will both be wrong, but you know what?"

"What?"

"It doesn't matter because that's what people do when they love each other."

A roar began inside his head, making it hard to hear. "Are you saying you love me?"

"I do. It killed me to think you didn't feel the same way about me. When you looked at me and pretended as if I wasn't anything more than a client to you...shit...I couldn't breathe." He shook his head. "Couldn't even function," he added. "Worst of all, I couldn't talk to you. I knew I would end up looking like an idiot because I love you so damn much. There is no way I could have kept it hidden, and I don't want to get trampled again. Being with you is all I've wanted since the moment we met. I'm tired of the pain and so sick of going without you."

"That reporter woman at the charity event said your reputation would be ruined if people learned about us. Your career is important to me because I know it is special to you. I did not wish to become an embarrassment."

At Asher's confession, a crazed light entered Rhys' eyes. Tucking Asher's body in as close as possible, Rhys went nose to nose with him. "I've never been as proud of anyone as I am of you. It's not your stupid, crazy high-priced clothing or your ridiculously gorgeous eyes. It's you. For all the massive outer beauty you possess, your inner beauty is phenomenal. You make me a better person."

There were no words.

"I mean look at you," Rhys continued. "Your clothes—which cost about a gazillion dollars more than mine— are soaked in your juices. I know you did that to keep me from getting dirty. Who even thinks that way? Why would you do those things?"

Asher drew his brows together.

"There is no sense in ruining your clothing. You are worth more than this. I always want to treat you with the care you deserve. My clothes mean nothing while you mean everything. Do you really wish to go home wet and sticky?"

"Uh, yeah, I do. When we're talking about this, I most certainly do."

Asher's confusion grew. "Why?"

Rhys' eyes turned wicked. "I love the feel of your jizz coating my skin. It turns me on. I'm proud of myself for owning your pleasure. I feel sexy when you get off on me."

Asher's mouth fell open. He couldn't stop it from happening. When he found his voice, he couldn't hold back. "You are always sexy. Do not dare tell me you do not know it. I have seen your 'I'm-the-most-charming-man-ever' act. You cannot lie to me."

A sad look passed over Rhys' features and he set Asher's clothes to rights. Once they were straight enough to make it home, Rhys reached up, taking Asher's face between his hands. Forcing him to hold his gaze, Rhys didn't hide a single thing from Asher. His eyes shone brightly with his every emotion as he spoke.

"Before you, I had nothing. I've never been loved by anyone other than my brothers. Even then, I didn't have them a majority of the time. We're all too broken. The only time I've ever been in love before meeting you, it did not end well for me." Rhys' eyes fell closed for a moment. He visibly swallowed before reopening his eyes. They'd become so sad, Asher wanted to close his own eyes to escape them. "Within a few short months of each other, my father killed himself, I realized the woman I loved did not love me in return, and we'd lost our baby." Rhys turned inside of himself for a moment. Blinking rapidly he eyes refocused. Wherever he'd gone, Asher didn't want him to ever go there again. He wanted to hold him. A baby? Asher's heart broke. The way he was with Adalyn told Asher everything. He would have been an amazing father.

"What happened to this woman who was to have your child?" Rhys' eyes went flat. "She married my brother the day I met you."

"Oh." He had nothing else. It explained so many things.

"I was angry and bitter when I met you." Rhys ran his fingers along Asher's jaw. Asher's skin tingled everywhere their skin touched. "In an instant, you changed everything. In a moment, when I thought I might drown, you saved me." His gaze became almost pleading as if begging Asher to understand. "You said you don't believe it, but I'm telling you it is true. There have been many, many times when I have looked in the mirror, and all I could see was an image of this broken, unwanted man."

Asher experienced a rush of fury. None of it aimed at Rhys. It was at a world that would allow a man such as him to feel unwanted for a single moment. "Get in the car, Rhys." Even to his ears, he sounded deadly.

Against his will, every muscle in his face had gone hard. There was no telling how it appeared to Rhys. He was powerless to stop it from happening. When Rhys didn't move, Asher repeated his order. It came out in a growl as he bit down on his rage. "Get in the car, Rhys."

Without questioning his reasons,

Rhys did as Asher demanded. The second Asher sat behind the wheel of the car he locked the doors. It was a ridiculous move. Rhys was a grown man. He could simply unlock the door and get out. Asher had done it to make a point. In case Rhys didn't understand, Asher cleared it up. Turning his head, he held Rhys' stare.

"You belong to me now. There has never been another man as sexy or as desired as you are, by me. We are going home. When we get there, I expect you nude and in our bed within five minutes." Asher started the car and worked his way out of the garage. "From there," he continued, "I intend to do many, many naughty things to your body. All of these things will end in several sticky fluids coating your body if you so wish, but you will know your worth afterward. Capisce?"

In an unexpected move, Rhys threw

322

his head back on a roar of laughter. Asher's eyebrows shot to his hairline. "Do you think I am joking?"

Out of the corner of his eye, he could see Rhys shaking his head. "I'm happy," he explained. "It's you. The things you do and say. They make me so fucking happy. Sometimes, it doesn't have anywhere to go and I have to let it out."

Rhys' answer soothed Asher's ire. It also made him realize how crazy he sounded. His shoulders relaxed. Swiping a tired hand over his eyes, he said the only thing he could think of that really mattered at all. "I love you, Rhys."

Rhys dropped his head back against the headrest. "I love you too, Asher."

Reaching over Rhys swiped his hand up Asher's thigh. He left it there. In that moment, Asher truly understood they would be okay. All the many confessions they'd made to one another throughout the life of their relationship still held true. Neither of them could or would stand without the other. They made it home, and everything Asher said came true.

The End

Keep an eye out for book 4, Unbalanced.

Author Bio

Charity Parkerson is an award winning and multi-published author with several companies. Born with no filter from her brain to her mouth, she decided to take this odd quirk and insert it in her characters.

*2015 Readers' Favorite Award Winner

*Winner of 2, 2014 Readers' Favorite Awards

*2015 Passionate Plume Award Finalist

*2013 Readers' Favorite Award Winner

*2013 Reviewers' Choice Award Winner

*2012 ARRA Finalist for Favorite Paranormal Romance

*Five-time winner of The Mistress of the Darkpath

Connect with her online:

--Website: charityparkerson.com

--Facebook:

facebook.com/authorCharityParkerson

facebook.com/TheMenofSin

--Twitter: twitter.com/CharityParkerso